THREADS OF BETRAYAL
CHRONICLES OF THE SOVEREIGNS
BOOK THREE

LANA J. WILLIAMS

COPYRIGHT

Copyright © 2026 by Lana J. Williams

All rights reserved.

No part of this book may be reproduced in any form or by any electronic or mechanical means, including information storage and retrieval systems, without written permission from the author, except for the use of brief quotations in a book review.

This novel is entirely a work of fiction. The names, characters and incidents portrayed in it are the work of the author's imagination. Any resemblance to actual persons, living or dead, events or localities is entirely coincidental.

Lana J. Williams asserts the moral right to be identified as the author of this work.

First edition

ISBN 9798993835631

For my father-in-law—you would've loved this one. As you said before, we will meet again. All of our threads will cross in the end.

BOOKS BY LANA J. WILLIAMS

<u>Chronicles of the Sovereigns</u>
Threads of Fate
The Mourner's Song (Prequel)
Threads of Betrayal

CONTENTS

	The Sovereigns	ix
	Part Two	1
1.	Eira	3
2.	Adrian	9
3.	Eira	14
4.	Eira	25
5.	Eira	34
6.	Eira	41
7.	Eira	50
8.	Eira	60
9.	Eira	64
10.	Eira	71
11.	Eira	85
12.	Eira	91
13.	The Loom *The Realm Reacts*	98
14.	Eira	106
15.	Adrian	114
16.	Eira & Adrian	119
17.	Eira & Adrian	123
18.	Eira	133
19.	Eira	140
20.	The Mortal Realm	152
21.	Eira	163
22.	The Architect	170
23.	Eira	173
	Epilogue- Adrian	179

Bonus Chapter - Death	183
Acknowledgements	187
About the Author	189

THE SOVEREIGNS

A list of The Sovereigns and their pronunciations.

1. Life – Zivael (*ZEE-vayl*)

2. Death – Thaloré (*THA-lor-ay*)

3. Mercy – Elestra (*eh-LESS-truh*)

4. Revenge – Vireth (*VEER-eth*)

5. Pleasure – Sedara (*seh-DAHR-uh*)

6. Pain – Akria (*ACK-ree-uh*)

7. Fury – Thamys (*THAH-miss*)

THE SOVEREIGNS

8. Peace – Eira (*AY-rah*)

9. Joy – Lysera (*lih-SAIR-uh*)

10. Sorrow – Melora (*meh-LOR-uh*)

11. Knowledge – Caelus *(KAY-luhs)*

PART TWO

The Becoming

CHAPTER 1
EIRA

Nothing about Eira's realm felt peaceful anymore. She could find no joy, no hope now that Adrian was with *them,* suffering at *their* hands. Or perhaps *they* suffered at *his*. She did not know, and she had not dared reach out to find him with her essence.

She stood barefoot at the edge of the water, hair loose around her shoulders, gown brushing softly against her skin. Eira's realm echoed her unrest, shifting to reflect her mood. The air thrummed softly, as if answering the beat of her heart.

She pressed her palm over her chest as she closed her eyes, thinking of *him*. The ache there had not dulled, and she did not think it ever would. It burned as fiercely as the day he was torn from her.

Adrian.

His name was both balm and blade, a solace to her chaos. She could still see his face when she closed her eyes. She pictured the curve of his smile, and his eyes that reminded her of dark pools of midnight. She couldn't help but conjure an image in her mind of the way he had looked at her as if she were the sum of all beginnings and endings. She had loved him in that small, impossible space where love and disobedience met, and now she bore the consequences.

But Adrian had lied. He lied about who he was, hid the truth of his blood behind those midnight eyes that held too much curiosity, too much love, too much *everything* to be contained in one man. That truth still bled, no matter how hard she tried to soften it with reason.

Eira turned from the water, anger flashing sharp beneath her grief. "You should have told me," she whispered into the wind. "You should have trusted me."

Her realm shuddered at her tone as a faint hum reverberated through the water. Eira knew it was a warning from Balance itself. Peace was not meant to feel wrath, for she was Peace. That was her nature, her duty. And in her disruption of balance, she had corrupted her very nature. Her anger threatened the very laws she embodied, but she could not stop feeling. She could not stop longing, wishing Adrian were here with her.

"He knew," she hissed to no one who could hear. "He knew what he was. He looked at me with mortal eyes while hiding the blood of a god. How dare he!"

"Would it have changed the outcome had he told you?" A voice came softly, carried on the still air.

Eira spun, eyes blazing with a mixture of fury and caution.

A tall figure stood where the horizon met the lake, robed in twilight, constellations sewn into the fabric of his mantle. His dark hair fell in loose obsidian waves to his shoulders, faint silver streaks glinting. His eyes held galaxies, and the vast knowledge of existence. Caelus—the forgotten brother, Sovereign of Knowledge.

A shiver ran through her as she stared at him, unease curling low in her stomach. "I remember you," Eira said slowly, stepping toward him. "But ... I do not. You were gone, and now you are here, and I do not know how I ever forgot you. How did I forget you, brother?"

Caelus tilted his head slightly, his expression unreadable. "Because you were made to forget, Eira."

Her pulse quickened and her brows scrunched as she stared into his eyes, looking for a hidden truth that was not yet revealed. "By whom?"

"The time is not right for you to hold that knowledge," Caelus said, his voice quiet but certain. "But I can tell you ... things have changed and the truth will be revealed soon."

Eira's throat tightened. "I am sure this must be dire if you have come back."

His lips curved faintly, not quite a smile. "Sister, it was always going to happen this way. No matter which path you chose."

He stepped closer, the constellations on his robe glinting faintly with each movement. "You once came to me for counsel, long ago. You asked if love could exist without consequence for us. I told you no, but you have always been curious. You are not the first."

Eira looked away, ashamed and defiant all at once. "Then tell me now, Caelus. What consequence comes of loving a demigod bound by The Fates? I cannot have him, and I do not know how to save him without starting a war."

She looked away, her eyes shining with silver tears. She couldn't banish the hurt, couldn't reconcile it with the love she still felt for him.

"I did not know," she said softly, setting her jaw. "I did not know what he truly was. I am so angry, brother."

Caelus' gaze softened. "You are not angry because of his omission, Eira. You are angry because he loved you enough to protect you from the truth."

Her breath hitched, a soft gasp escaping as the truth of his words pierced the place where love still lingered. Caelus stepped closer, his presence strangely comforting.

"He hid what he was so you would not bear the weight of what that meant. His blood is prophecy, and his heart is light. Adrian could be considered a weapon because his blood has ties to the old gods, but I do not believe he was ever a weapon forged against you."

Eira met his eyes, her fury dissolving into confusion. "How can I get him back? How can I release him from The Three Fates?"

Caelus looked out over the water, his expression distant. "That is best discussed another time. And right now, I do not have much of it."

The water rippled violently, light flashing beneath its surface as Eira took a step back, her gown sweeping around her legs. "Can Adrian be freed? Could I go to him now?"

"Perhaps," Caelus said, his voice barely a whisper. "But if you try, you may very well destroy Balance in the process."

"I would destroy everything that keeps him from me," Eira said sharply, clenching her fists as she lifted her face to the sky. The golden threads shimmered overhead, glinting as though answering her defiance.

Caelus smiled, not a true smile, but a sorrowful curve of his lips. "You sound like you mean that."

"I don't think I've ever spoken truer words," she said, her voice low but firm.

They stood in silence for a long moment, watching the light tremble on the water. Then Eira asked, softer, "Why did I forget you, Caelus? Truly?"

He turned to her, his eyes vast and knowing. "Because when I left, I took the memory with me. That is all I can say."

"What did you know?" she whispered.

"I know all things. But would it change anything if you knew?" he said gently. "Sometimes it is best to let things unfold the way they were intended."

Eira felt something inside her fracture. This uncertainty was foreign to her and she was out of patience, tired of waiting.

"Tell me what I have to become to save him," she murmured, looking off. "I cannot be Peace when my heart is in ruin. Who must I become, Caelus?"

Caelus' voice lowered as he looked to the sky, then back at her. "Something more than Peace. More than what your nature allows you to be."

When Eira looked back, he was gone. Only fragments of starlight remained, dissolving into the air. She stood alone, her reflection rippling in the lake. The horizon quivered faintly, as if the world itself knew what was to come.

"If I must become something more," she whispered, "then heavens help the ones who caused it."

CHAPTER 2
ADRIAN

The Loom shuddered as Adrian explored its endless expanse. Every thread within sight rippled outward, creating an ocean of light and shadow folding over itself. Adrian stood unmoving at its center, radiating golden light.

"So what will you show me now that you know you can't keep me?" His voice was low but carried throughout the expanse. "Show me the cost. Let me see the world you guard so desperately."

The threads flared to life instantly, obeying his command. The Loom answered to no one, yet it wanted Adrian to see. It was eager to show him what was to come.

Scenes poured through the threads, flashing across Adrian's mind. There were millions of lives stitched into the same endless fabric, each following their own thread. He saw what had been, and what was yet to come—and he watched, unmoving.

The tapestry pulsed with heartbeat after heartbeat until it was almost too much to bear. But Adrian endured. He *would* endure, for he was no mere mortal. He was born of the blood of gods.

"This is what you will break if you stay on your path," The Loom whispered. Its voice rumbled like thunder pressed through glass. It was impossible to locate, woven through every thread, seeping into his thoughts.

"Every breath, every name, every moment. You risk destroying Balance."

Golden light burned in Adrian's eyes as they hardened with resolve. "Maybe the world would be better off without your leash."

"Without design there is nothing. Chaos does not nurture, child of light. It devours. And we will not allow that."

Adrian's jaw set, anger simmering just beneath the surface. "You will not hold me, and I WILL get back to Eira."

"She is being undone by you. By your very existence," The Loom whispered.

"She will be *freed* by me," he said, closing his eyes against the storm of light.

The Loom's vibration deepened until the light around him became a wrathful storm. Threads lashed through the air like whips striking toward him, but Adrian would not yield. He lifted his arm and the blows scattered against a flare of golden light that burst from his skin.

"I will not bow," he said. "Not to you. Not to your Architect."

"Balance is order. Order is survival," The Loom hissed.

"Then maybe survival isn't enough," Adrian shot back, defiantly.

The air cracked and the web of threads drew itself tight, pulling in until every strand converged on him, binding him in living light. His limbs locked and his breath left him in a gasp. But Adrian was resilient; he had to be. The blood of Apollo ran in his veins, and he would not be silenced as the old gods were.

"You are not the first to defy Balance," The Loom's voice vibrated throughout him. *"The old gods were banished for it. The Architect bound them to keep the world from dissolving. Surely you know this, child of light. When you tamper with Balance there is always a price."*

"And yet, here I am," Adrian rasped, struggling against the bindings. "You couldn't erase *me*."

The threads tightened, holding him in place.

"I will go to Eira," he whispered, gritting his teeth. "She is mine." The sound of her name broke the silence like a stone shattering glass.

The Loom hesitated until the bindings loosened an

infinitesimal amount. *"You would destroy the world for her?"*

"I would destroy the world for the *choice* to be with her," Adrian said firmly, golden light spilling between the threads that held him. "For the right to love without asking permission."

"If you cling to her," the voice said, caressing his thoughts, *"you will risk everything. All will burn."*

"Then let it burn. Let us all feel the consequences of suppressing free will," Adrian said, and meant every word.

Lines of pure light snapped free and recoiled, like veins ripped from a beating heart. For a moment, the whole structure seemed to falter, and in the distance he saw Eira's realm, trembling and unbalanced; on the very edge of collapse.

Adrian reached for it instinctively, heart twisting as he saw her move gracefully within her realm. Her face gentled the fury blazing in his veins, calmed the storm that was rising. The threads between them blazed white-hot, pain searing through every nerve as he fought to touch the vision shimmering before him. Pain roared through him, but he did not stop. He HAD to get to her. She was his, and he was hers.

"You cannot touch her!" The Loom thundered.

"I already have. I have touched her here," Adrian said softly, placing a hand across his heart.

"Then you have chosen," The Loom said, the voice

caressing his mind. *"You are their destruction. Your mere existence threatens the Sovereigns."*

The threads released him abruptly and Adrian inhaled sharply as he collapsed to his knees. The echo of The Loom's words rang throughout the infinite chamber.

"Things can change," Adrian said, staring at Eira's reflection.

"We have seen the end. We know what is coming and we will not warn you again," it hissed, many voices yet one.

Adrian raised his head, defiantly. "That is a problem we will deal with later."

The light surged, pulsing furiously, and then it vanished. Darkness swept over him, vast and eternal. The threads were still, dimmed to dull gold as he looked around, expecting to hear the voice again. He did not.

Adrian rose slowly and straightened his shoulders, every line of him blazing with golden light. The mortal softness he carried was gone; what remained was the poise of divinity tempered by grief and anger. He looked upward into the endless weave.

"I will find you," he said quietly, holding Eira's image in his mind. He had memorized the sadness in her eyes, the fracture in her realm, and he knew he would have to go to her.

"I will fix this."

CHAPTER 3
EIRA

In her realm, Eira's waters rippled in spirals instead of circles, as if stirred by a hand she could not see. The soft light that once rested over the horizon pulsed faintly, a sign that Balance was watching. Balance was vigilant, always looming, and the unrest she felt at the shift had been so unsettling she could feel the weight of it.

The willows by her waters swayed slightly, possibly feeling the disruption in her realm. She sensed his absence, as though he had always been a part of her realm. She stood there, mind racing with thoughts of *him* as if she could bring him to her. She wished she could. She should be able to ... but she could not.

Eira could feel Adrian's presence lingering like a

soft touch, caressing the recesses of her mind. Since he was taken from her, he had consumed her thoughts constantly, residing in a space where duty and longing warred daily. As badly as she wanted to go to him, she knew the risk was too great, even for her. It was too great for all of her siblings, and she would not be the final break to end the Sovereigns.

Lately it felt as though her realm were Peace in name only. Everything around her was unraveling, remnants of what used to be before her violation. Before her trespass. She inhaled shakily, fingers curling at her sides as she tried to steady the storm raging inside her. Every attempt to calm her realm only made it shudder harder, as though resisting her touch. It was almost as if her realm were resisting *her*. And maybe it was resisting her very presence ... or at least what she was becoming while her nature was disturbed.

"I know," she whispered into the trembling air, steadying herself. "I feel it too. I wish I could calm it."

A ripple of shadow appeared at her back and Eira knew the shadow before she heard the voice that accompanied it. She could feel her siblings' presence as soon as they entered her realm and knew instinctually who it was. His energy was raw and powerful, suffocating the air in her realm.

"Your pain is louder than you realize, sister. I could

feel your presence through my domain," the voice said, causing her waters to calm as if he commanded them. Even the water in Eira's realm steadied for the Sovereign who was Death.

Thaloré stepped beside her, silent as a breath from the dead. The cold, dark beauty that was Death oozed the type of power that held dominion over everything his essence touched, even here. But Eira knew that he could not undo what had been done. Even Death could not contain what had been unleashed by the disruption of Balance.

He studied her with an unblinking, unreadable gaze before he spoke. "Your essence is shifting, sister," he said as his eyes roamed over her, assessing.

Eira swallowed, her gaze meeting his steely gray one. "Yes, I can feel the change, brother. Balance doesn't answer me the way it once did." She lowered her head before returning her gaze to meet his. "Perhaps what I did was the ultimate violation."

"It is not Balance that has changed," Thaloré murmured, never breaking eye contact. "It is you, Eira. *You* are changing."

The lake throbbed beneath them, light shivering up from its depths in waves that mirrored her racing heart. Eira sank to her knees at the water's edge and pressed both palms to its cool surface, searching for the familiar pull of her realm—her place of solace. But even here, where the land bent instinctively to her will and the grass bowed beneath her touch, she knew there would be no relief.

"I cannot make it stop," she whispered as a tear slipped down her cheek. "I cannot quiet anything, Thaloré. Not my thoughts. Not this grief. Not this ... anger. And I am so, so very angry."

Her voice broke as her hands balled to fists. The reflection beneath her eyes warped, sensing her turmoil.

"I am Peace. I am not supposed to feel this much!" Eira's shout sent the air rippling outward. "Look what I have done!"

The ground began to shake as a quiet sob tore free from her. Death lowered himself beside her, robes pooling like shadows around them.

"Peace is not the absence of feeling," Thaloré said quietly, placing a hand over hers for comfort. "It is the mastery of it. But you, sister ... " he paused, and for the first time, she heard something like hesitation in his voice, "you are unraveling as the days pass."

Eira flinched as if she had been struck. "I am failing my nature? Then what am I, brother? What am I, if not Peace?"

Thaloré steadied her trembling hand, his voice gentle. "You are peace. But ... you are outgrowing it."

A sharp exhale escaped her. "Thaloré ... " She stared at her trembling hands. "What am I becoming?"

He did not answer immediately. His gaze drifted

over her realm as he took in the erratic shimmer of the horizon, the vibrating air, and the rippling water that refused to be still.

"Peace cannot hold anger," he finally said. "It dissolves under it. You have held rage in your heart for too long, Eira. Love amplified it. But your loss has honed it into something sharp, something *different*. And now what remains is ... something new."

A chill slid through her as she let his words settle. She knew his words held truth, but the implications of that truth were realm altering. World shattering. Eira wanted so many things. She wanted to free Adrian ... to restore Balance ... to be free from the restraints of it all. She had never resented her duty or her nature but lately that had begun to change. Lately she desired things that a Sovereign should not.

"New," Eira said, echoing Thaloré's words as she swirled her hand in the water, "or forbidden?"

His eyes flickered, and for a heartbeat she saw fear in him. She had never known Thaloré to fear anything, but the shift in his demeanor confirmed that whatever was happening would change everything.

"There is a name for this, brother," Eira said slowly, straightening to meet his gaze. "What I am feeling—this does not feel like peace. It feels like ... chaos."

She clenched her fist, unease sliding up her spine

like a cold wind. She barely wanted to give the word shape, afraid that speaking it aloud would make it real.

Thaloré inhaled sharply and caught her hand before she could pull away. His grip was firm but gentle, steadying her racing mind.

"Chaos has no Sovereign," he said quietly. "It never has. And it never should. If it were meant to be, that would have been the design—but it was not."

Eira let his words sink in. That did not mean it could never have one—only that it never had. Sensing her thoughts, the lake split beneath them in a jagged line, the water recoiling as if struck. Eira staggered back, thrusting out a hand to still it.

"No," she hissed, a pulse of her essence rippling outward through the realm. "No—that isn't what I meant. I would never. That is not my nature."

The water shuddered but did not obey her, its currents quickening as if propelled by a strong wind. Her realm was rejecting her, slowly but unmistakably, refusing to steady at her command. The realization unsettled her. Eira knew what was coming—it was unavoidable.

"You are already changing," Thaloré said gently, a sigh slipping from him as if in defeat. "Your realm is proof, sister. Balance will soon cease to recognize you as you are."

Tears burned her eyes but she wiped them away, squaring her shoulders as she stood. Eira pressed a hand against her heart, trying to steady the pounding inside.

"If I lose myself, I lose him, Thaloré," she exhaled, tipping her head back to stare at the golden threads pulsing overhead. "I will not lose him."

"If you do not stop this change," Thaloré said quietly, "you lose everything. I do not want that for you, sister. We have all suffered enough due to our choices." He turned away then, his expression closed off as if the weight of old memories had returned. His expression looked almost pained, and Eira wondered what losses Death himself had endured.

Eira stilled as her mind wandered to spaces it shouldn't. "There must be a way to stop this."

"Not to stop," Thaloré corrected softly. "To understand."

He rose and offered his hand. Eira took it, inclining her head in acceptance.

"There was a woman once … " Thaloré began, his eyes searching Eira's as his expression softened, "a very long time ago. Her name was Lenora." He spoke the name reverently, as though it had once been sacred to him.

Thaloré straightened, his jaw tightening as his gaze drifted into the distance, and Eira felt herself stiffen in response. She did not know what he was about to reveal, only that it carried deep emotional weight.

"I loved her. Very dearly," he said, a brief flash of pain crossing his face. "She was mortal. Her thread—" he reached out, fingers curling as though he could still feel it, "it called to me. I followed it until I found her. I tried to stay away, but Lenora was powerful enough to make me defy The Fates."

His voice faltered. "And she paid for that. I will always carry the burden of losing her, because I could have prevented it by staying away."

A single tear traced a path down his pale, striking face. He brushed it away, studying the moisture on his fingertips as though it were unfamiliar.

Eira stepped closer and placed a gentle hand on Thaloré's shoulder, wishing she could offer him peace. But she understood loss too well to believe such wounds could truly be healed.

"I never knew," she said quietly. "I am sorry, brother. To love and then lose it—I would not wish that pain on anyone."

Death inclined his head in acknowledgment, recognizing the grief they shared before he spoke again.

"Go to Sedara," he said as he released her hand and stepped back. "She might be able to better help you understand your situation … " he looked at her knowingly before continuing, "and The Void."

Eira recoiled. She had no desire to see her sister, especially after their last encounter. "Pleasure? What would she know of The Void? And how would that help me, Thaloré?"

"The Void," he started, voice regaining its commanding tone, "is where chaos first took form. And Sedara was imprisoned there for her transgressions. It is not a place fit for a Sovereign."

Eira's breath caught at the thought of Sedara being imprisoned. She had always known Sedara had *gone* for awhile—that her sister had vanished beyond the veils and returned altered, dangerous in new ways. Sovereigns came and went, as was their nature. Absence was not unusual among them. But this was not absence—it was punishment, and the knowledge burned, stirring a deep, unfamiliar anger within her.

"So she wasn't just gone," Eira said quietly. "She was punished ... like the old gods." Her voice faltered. "This was unknown to me."

Thaloré inclined his head. "In a way, yes."

Eira did not need the rest spoken aloud. The old gods' fate was well known to all of them. She knew they had been unmade by The Architect and cast into The Chasm, their essence sealed away so the universe could endure. That truth had never been hidden.

But Sedara had not been unmade. She had been condemned—and returned.

"Sedara tasted the forbidden once," Thaloré

said, watching as Eira's expression changed to pity. "She endured what you may have to survive. If anyone can tell you where this path leads, it is her."

The lake trembled again, harder this time, and the horizon flickered, drawing both of their attention. Eira closed her eyes and reached outward with her essence, because she *knew* he was there. She knew he was close, yet impossibly far beyond her reach. The knowledge was maddening.

Eira felt Adrian across worlds. Her heart called to him, unrelenting, and she knew that might have been the first fracture—the wound that had never healed. She could also feel the break that her realm couldn't hide. And she understood, with quiet certainty, that it would be her undoing.

She opened her eyes and nodded once, staring at her brother. "I will go to her."

Thaloré's expression did not change, but the faintest shift in the air told her he approved. "Eira," he said as she turned to leave.

She paused, waiting for him to speak.

"What you are becoming," he said quietly, "does not have to be destruction."

Her pulse stilled for a moment, considering what he was saying.

"It can be power," he finished—and then he was gone.

The words sank deep, hitting their mark. What Death spoke of was dangerous and tempting, but true.

Eira stepped away, determination burning beneath her grief. She knew what she had to do, a plan forming in her mind as she crossed the veil to venture to Pleasure's realm.

The moment she left, the lake cracked like glass.

CHAPTER 4
EIRA

Pleasure's realm was always too warm, always too sweet. The air was thick with perfume and lust, a suffocating mix. Eira stepped through the veil and felt the air drape itself around her like silk, scented with figs, wine, and something darker. The air here tasted like sin.

The sky was perpetual dusk, blushed in gold and violet. Lanterns drifted between the palms like stars, brightening the sky. Soft, intoxicating music hummed beneath everything, moving across her skin in gentle vibrations.

Sedara had always used beauty like a weapon, and her realm reflected it. Rich velvets and vibrant satin draped every surface, their softness deliberate, concealing the unyielding granite beneath. The air was heavy with indulgence, wrapped in sinful delights meant to disarm and invite. But Eira knew better. Beneath the elegance lay something barbed and unforgiving, a reminder that this beauty was not meant to comfort—it was meant to ensnare.

Eira walked across the marble terrace, each step stirring rose petals whose scents wafted up to her nose. Eira noted that the world seemed to shift for her, recognizing a Sovereign ... and something else; something unfamiliar that stirred beneath her skin. She wasn't surprised. Her realm always responded to her siblings' presence. But this welcome felt entirely different.

A low, melodic voice purred from the shadows, drawing her attention. "Peace, what a pleasant surprise."

Sedara emerged with a lazy grace, draped in a long burgundy gown that clung to her like a second skin, the fabric curving deliberately over her lush figure before spilling into a slow, liquid fall at her feet. The neckline dipped just enough to be distracting, showing her voluptuous breasts. It was the kind of dress that promised pleasure and consequences in equal measure.

Her red hair, once sleek and controlled, now cascaded in vibrant, bouncing curls, glinting with gold dust, that framed her face and brushed her bare shoulders with every movement. Her lips were painted a deep, decadent red, full and pouty, curved in a sweet smile edged with venom. Eira knew her sister well enough to sense that Sedara meant no harm—at least not today.

The moment Sedara's eyes found Eira, they sharpened, dissecting her outward appearance before piercing through to her very essence.

"Oh." Sedara stepped closer, her expression twisting as she traced the fractures in Eira's form. "You're cracking." Her nose wrinkled in distaste, gaze roaming over Eira as if she were a fine vase shattered beyond repair.

Eira bristled, offended by her sister's words. "I don't need commentary, Sedara." She shifted uncomfortably, narrowing her eyes. Sedara had a way of honing her words into blades, and she never swung them unless she intended to cut.

"You never did like honesty," Sedara murmured, a smug curl to her lips as she circled her. "You always preferred stillness. Control. Tell me, sister, how is that working for you?"

Sedara tapped a perfectly manicured finger against Eira's temple. "It looks like you're losing both. And so is Peace."

Eira swallowed hard as she swatted Sedara's hand away, a sharp retort poised on the edge of her tongue. "I did not come here to be mocked. I came because—"

"You came here because I am the only Sovereign who's ever—" Sedara leaned in closer, perfume infiltrating Eira's senses, her smile wicked, "been imprisoned in The Void and returned."

Her last words lingered, settling heavily over Eira. It was true. Sedara was the only Sovereign—perhaps the only entity—to enter The Void and return. The question was not how Sedara had survived. It was how she had known that was what Eira had come for.

Eira's pulse hammered. "Tell me how to enter The Void and come back with him," she demanded.

Sedara arched a brow, her smile slow and knowing. "Not *how*, dear heart. *Where.*" She leaned closer, voice dripping with sweetness. "The Void is a realm between realms. It lies within The Chasm, where what is unmade does not always disappear cleanly."

She turned away toward the dark horizon, lost in memory. "You fall," Sedara murmured. "Past fate. Past memory. Past everything you are. The Void strips you down to what you are willing to keep."

Sedara walked toward the balcony, her steps unhurried, until the marble opened onto a vast expanse of starlit black water that stretched endlessly below, its surface gleaming like spilled night.

"The Void is chaos incarnate. It's endless and hungry. I tasted it while I was suspended in its vastness for an age. I wish to never go back. It was not the most ... *pleasant* ... experience." Sedara looked on, lost in a place Eira could not reach. Possibly a memory from long ago.

"And Adrian?" Eira asked quietly. "Is that where The Fates are holding him?" She said their name with measured precision, the fury beneath it sharp enough to cut.

Sedara exhaled slowly, gazing out over the dark waters. "No. The Three keep their prisoners close, tangled in The Loom, bound by their own threads. *Assuming* Adrian is a prisoner ... " she trailed off, slyly.

Eira shifted, her jaw tightening at Sedara's words. "I will not go back to The Gates," Eira said, cold fury simmering in her eyes. "I will not kneel before them again."

Sedara's smile returned, slow and approving. "I wouldn't expect you to."

She stepped closer, the air between them warming, her amusement giving way to something far more deliberate. "Listen to me, sister," Sedara said, lowering her voice as the lanterns around them dimmed to conspiratorial haze. "There is a door at the edge of The Void. A tear in the fabric. If you want to reach Adrian, you will need to enter that breach. It is the only way that does not pass through The Gates."

Sedara tilted her head, eyes assessing. "You should understand this, sister—the path to him will not be easy. The Fates are not kind, and they do not bargain. They will have little interest in negotiating with you, given your ... recent transgressions. But you already know this."

Eira's stomach dropped, a cold unease settling deep in her chest. Fear pricked at her senses, sharp and unwelcome, yet she leaned closer all the same.

"Sedara, what would they want with him? His bloodline is gone, so why *him*? He is half mortal."

Sedara's expression shifted, the faintest trace of pity surfacing—enough to make Eira recoil. She wanted no sympathy, and had not come to be comforted. She had come to reclaim what had been taken from her. To free the mortal—no, the demigod —who had slipped quietly into her heart and held it captive.

"They want what he is, sister. A demigod born of Apollo's bloodline. If influenced, he could be capable of great or terrible things. It will depend on which path he chooses."

She tilted her head, thoughtful, a faint smirk playing at her lips. "Personally," she added, "I hope he destroys them. Adrian might very well be able to rewrite fate."

Eira's throat tightened as she thought of the implications in Sedara's words. "Adrian wouldn't … " She stopped, leaving the sentence hanging between them like an echo on a dying wind. Eira wasn't sure which path Adrian would choose, or whether he would ever find his way back to her.

Sedara's gaze searched Eira's for a moment before she spoke. "Have you felt it? A shift in your nature?"

Eira shut her eyes, shame rising like heat. "Yes. But I do not acknowledge it."

Sedara studied her for a long moment, eyes dark and intent. "It is awakening in you," she said evenly. "And you will not be able to deny it when it consumes. You would be wise to accept it before that moment comes, Eira."

Eira opened her eyes, her voice calm despite the storm beneath it. "I don't want it. I just want him back."

"Oh, Eira." For once, Sedara did not smile. Her voice softened, and the absence of amusement carried a seriousness that did not go unnoticed. "That's exactly why you *will* become it."

The truth hit like a blow to the heart. Sedara lifted a hand and pressed it lightly over Eira's heart.

"You feel him through the threads, don't you? Even now."

Eira's voice was a whisper as she answered. "Yes."

Sedara looked at her long and hard. "I survived The Void," Sedara said quietly, "because I desired something fiercely enough to keep my Sovereignty."

"But," Sedara continued, voice shifting into something more serious than Eira had ever heard from her, "love can be weapon and shield both. If you cling to yourself, you may come out changed—but alive."

"And Adrian?" Eira whispered.

Sedara's mouth tightened. "If you reach him, you

may be able to bring him back from whatever he has become."

Eira's knees nearly buckled as she braced against the balcony railing. Sedara moved quickly, gently supporting her arm.

"Look at me, Eira," Sedara said softly.

Eira turned to face her.

"You need to understand this: The Fates will not give Adrian freely," Sedara continued, "and once you decide—that decision will be final. Are you willing to die, Peace?" Sedara's gaze was bright with a dangerous clarity.

She did not answer, and Sedara stepped closer, caressing a strand of Eira's loose hair. Then the world went silent. It was the absence of sound completely. The low hum of the realm vanished, the whisper of wind stilled, even the distant surge of the dark sea below fell mute. The absence pressed in on Eira's ears until it rang, a crushing quiet that made her own breath sound too loud. Then the marble beneath their feet groaned.

A fracture split the terrace with a sharp, echoing crack, racing outward like lightning trapped in stone. The rose petals scattered, lifting into the air as if caught in a sudden, directionless wind. Above them, the sky dimmed and shifted, the gold threads vibrating as though disturbed by an invisible hand.

Sedara stilled, lifting her gaze to the sky. Her

expression sharpened, eyes narrowing with sudden alertness.

"Well," she murmured, withdrawing her hand, "that didn't take long." Her eyes narrowed, distaste curling her lips.

Eira froze. She had not spoken her thoughts aloud. She had not *decided* anything. Yet the realm had answered. The golden threads overhead flickered violently now, snapping taut before loosening and Eira felt it in her bones. It felt uncomfortably like recognition.

Sedara exhaled a soft, humorless laugh. "Careful, sister," she said lightly. "You're thinking too loudly. I'm sure *they* can hear you."

Eira turned, heart pounding. "I did not do this."

"No," Sedara agreed, her eyes locking onto Eira's. "You didn't."

Another tremor rolled through the terrace, subtle but unmistakable. Somewhere far beyond the veil, something stirred, attentive.

Sedara's smile returned, slower this time, edged with interest. "But it appears The Loom heard you."

Eira's fingers curled at her sides as the truth settled heavy inside her. She had not reached for Adrian. She had not named the choice aloud. But her heart had. And the universe, it seemed, was already bracing for what that might mean.

CHAPTER 5
EIRA

The path from Sedara's realm dissolved beneath Eira's feet the moment she stepped away from the velvet dusk. There was no gentle return to still water and pale light, nor a familiar horizon waiting to receive her.

The world shifted into cold, heavy shadow. Eira stood in the realm between veils, an empty vastness that pressed in on her senses where nothing lived nor lingered. Her heart tightened as the air pressed in around her, thick with a gravity that had nothing to do with weight. This was not The Void, but it lay close enough to it that her skin prickled in warning. A faint whisper curled around her ankles like smoke, curious.

She forced it back. *Not yet.* She could feel it now—something coiled and impatient, waiting for her to challenge it. Eira clenched her jaw, resisting the urge to.

Raising her hand, she spoke a command in an ancient language, fed by memory and instinct. Pure white light split the darkness, opening a narrow door that spiraled upward. She stepped through.

The shadow thinned as she ascended, loosening its grip until the pressure in her chest eased. With each step, the darkness gave way to something vast and precise, until the path ended.

Eira emerged into an open expanse of constellations, and for a moment she forgot to breathe. This realm was nothing like her other siblings'. Stars stretched endlessly in every direction, not scattered, but arranged with deliberate intent. Their patterns were too intricate to be random, pulsing faintly as though responding to an unseen order. There was no horizon nor sky, only distance and awareness.

This was Knowledge's domain.

Empty—not in absence, but in restraint. Here, nothing demanded her attention. Nothing sought to seduce or command her. Even her own presence did not disturb it; Peace was not required here. It simply remained.

Eira took a cautious step forward. Grass met her bare feet, cool and soft, threaded with silver dew that reflected the constellations above. Trees rose nearby, their branches arching gently, leaves shimmering as though woven from starlight.

At the center of the clearing stood a small house, warmly lit from within. It was unmistakably mortal in its design—plain, familiar, and utterly out of place among the stars. She was taken aback at the sight of it. Of all the forms Knowledge might have chosen—endless archives, towering halls of record—this felt intentional in a way that warmed her. This place felt as though Caelus had shaped his realm not to display knowledge, but to remember it.

"You came sooner than I expected," a calm voice spoke from behind her, and Eira turned.

Caelus stood a short distance away, the constellations subtly shifting around him, aligning as though drawn by his gravity. Galaxies swirled in his silver eyes, truths layered upon truths.

"If Sedara and Thaloré gave you answers," Caelus said, studying her with unnerving clarity, "why have you come to me?"

Eira met his gaze, holding it despite the intensity behind it.

"Because answers are no longer enough," she said. "I need to understand in order to decide."

Caelus regarded her, tilting his head in contemplation before he spoke. "Ah, your quest for knowledge," he said quietly.

Eira stiffened, measuring her next words. "Tell me about the old gods."

The stars dimmed. Not all at once—just enough for her to notice. She knew whatever came next would shape every decision that followed.

Caelus did not answer at once.

"He unmade them," Caelus said at last. "The Architect stripped them of form. Of name. Of continuity. He severed them from the threads of existence and cast what remained into The Chasm. But you know this."

Eira did not bristle. She held his gaze. "I know what happened to the old gods," she said. The stars dimmed slightly, as if in confirmation. "What I do not know," she continued, "is *why* they were sent *there* and not to The Void like Sedara."

Caelus's expression sharpened, interest flickering behind his calm.

"The Void is punishment," Caelus said quietly. "The Chasm is something else entirely."

She stepped closer, bare feet brushing the dew-bright grass. "Tell me why the old gods were given to The Chasm instead of The Void."

Understanding dawned in Caelus' eyes, the stars within them swirling furiously. "You are not asking about them," he said.

"No," Eira replied. Her voice was steady, but something coiled beneath it. "I am asking about myself."

The constellations shifted again, rearranging their patterns.

"The old gods embodied chaos," Caelus began, "not consequence-born chaos, but origin chaos; endless creation without restraint. The Void could not contain them—it would have fed them. So The Architect gave them to The Chasm instead."

"To be held," Eira whispered.

"Yes," Caelus said. "Contained. Unraveling without return. The Chasm does not devour. It *keeps*."

Eira's hand curled at her side. "And The Void?"

"The Void strips," he said. "It breaks form but leaves something behind. That is why Sedara survived it. And why she returned."

Eira considered his words before replying. "So if I continue down this path ... "

Caelus regarded her for a long moment, as though choosing his words.

"You will not be treated as the old gods were," he said. "You are not origin chaos. You are Balance-born. And if I were to guess—one of The Architect's most prized creations."

Her heart pounded, but she continued to listen.

"But if Peace collapses entirely," he continued, "and a new form takes its place unchecked—then yes. You risk becoming something the universe will no longer punish."

The words settled like frost, yet Eira remained still

as he spoke. "You risk becoming something it will seek to contain."

Silence stretched between them, vast and waiting.

Eira lifted her chin. "They will seek to keep me in The Chasm, just like the old gods."

Caelus did not deny it, and that was confirmation enough.

"The old gods' rebellion cracked The Loom for the first time," Caelus said. "From that fracture, something else was born. There have been quite a few fractures. And now ... something else is taking shape."

"Peace," Caelus said gently, "was created in answer to it. You were not made merely to soothe mortals," he continued, his voice steady but heavy with regret. "You were made to temper chaos itself. To keep creation from collapsing."

Her eyes widened a fraction as the truth settled into place. "This is why my nature is ... changing."

Caelus' expression softened—and the sight of it terrified her.

"Peace cannot withstand grief or anger," he said quietly. "And you have endured more than you were designed to bear."

A question burned on the edge of her tongue, and she dared to ask the question. "Caelus, can *they* be overthrown?"

" ... Yes," he said at last. "But only by one thing."

"What?" she whispered.

"By someone powerful enough to take their place. You know that there is always a cost."

Something inside her unfurled, wild and burning. Caelus stepped forward and cupped her cheek, his touch cool and reassuring.

"You are becoming exactly what the world feared you could be," he said softly. "And exactly what you *need* to be if you intend to save Adrian."

Tears slipped down her face as she looked off into the distance. "But that is not my nature."

"Then be something new," Caelus replied. "Something The Loom never accounted for."

Eira lifted her gaze. "And The Fates?"

Caelus smiled, and it was cold, and lethal. "They have grown complacent, sister," he said. "They have forgotten that even destiny can bleed. If you intend to challenge them, you must delve deeper."

Eira nodded, resolve settling like fire in her bones. To save Adrian ... to stop the unraveling ... to reclaim herself ... she would face The Void. She would face The Fates and whatever she was becoming. Peace was breaking, and in it's place something was rising.

Eira only hoped she would survive it.

CHAPTER 6
EIRA

Eira had not returned to the mortal realm since the night Adrian was taken from her. She had felt no pull toward it; no curiosity, nor longing. A world that no longer held him had nothing left to offer her.

Now, as her feet touched the pavement, the ache in her chest flared sharp and sudden, as if something inside her had been torn open and exposed to the air. It pressed in on her lungs, relentless, unbearable in its weight. For a moment, she wondered if she had misjudged herself and if coming here had been a mistake.

She had expected the world to feel unchanged. The same restless movement, the same sleepless hum mortals called life. Instead, it was overwhelming; too loud, too alive. Every sound pressed against her senses with insistent force, as if the city itself were demanding her attention. Once, that vibrancy had drawn her in and fascinated her. Now, it made her want to retreat.

Mortality always carried a certain chaos, but now it pressed against her skin like a reminder that she wasn't meant to linger here anymore. Not as she was becoming.

She walked without making a sound, feet carrying her through the familiar streets, body remembering the way without her directing it. Every window she passed reflected fragments of her that did not match —golden eyes flashing where they shouldn't, shadows bending around her as if bowing. But Peace did not command shadows. Another entity entirely did. She forced the thought away and kept moving.

Adrian's building rose before her, ordinary and unremarkable. A place that normally would not have mattered to her—except that it had been his. The place he lived, breathed, and dreamed. And now he was gone, and the world felt emptier because of it.

Eira closed her eyes and the street vanished. She stood in his apartment, breath catching as his presence pressed in from every direction. The quiet was intimate yet invasive, making her feel like an uninvited guest in a space that had once been alive.

The scent of cedar and rain hit her first, then the faint trace of paint from the canvases scattered around the room. Shadows clung to the corners, but everything else was exactly as he'd left it. His mug was still on the counter and his jacket hung on the chair. It was as if he had stepped out for air and would return at any moment.

Eira walked deeper into the room, her fingers brushing the back of the couch, the edge of the sketchbook, and the worn spine of a book she had watched him read. Each point of contact sent a sharp pulse through her heart, pain blooming almost debilitating her.

This was the last place she had held him. The last place he had been *Adrian* and not a weapon or a prisoner. Regret constricted her lungs; she should have given in sooner. She should have stolen more time, demanded more moments. Instead, she had hesitated, cautious and restrained. Now … she was left only with memories that pressed in from all sides.

She sank into the chair beside his desk, fingers curling around the edge as if anchoring herself to something solid might keep her from unraveling. She leaned forward, resting her forehead against her hands, and forced herself to breathe.

"Adrian … " she breathed his name, willing her voice not to crack, "I am here."

The room answered with silence, as she knew it would. But the threads did not. A faint shimmer rippled through the air, fragile, like the tremor of a spiderweb caught in wind. Eira lifted her head sharply, eyes focused on the movement. A golden thread cut through the room, flickering at the edge of sight.

Adrian. It had to be. She reached for it.

Pain shot through her fingers like lightning, burning so sharply she gasped and dropped her hand. Her palm flashed with white-hot, searing pain. Pushing beyond it, she sent her essence to the thread, searching for Adrian.

He was too far away, held somewhere no mortal space could reach. But she felt him. She felt the echo of his stubbornness. And almost—*almost*—the rhythmic pulse of his heartbeat.

Tears blurred her vision and she wiped them away, smiling as she closed her eyes.

"You are alive," she whispered. "You are alive, I can feel you."

The golden thread pulsed once, in answer, but it was not enough for a message. Not enough to show her where he was. But it was something. It was just enough to remind her he was still fighting.

Eira rose slowly, wiping the tears from her cheeks. Pain still hummed under her skin, but purpose coiled beneath it.

"Listen to me," she whispered to the thread, knowing he could not hear her—not yet. "I won't let them keep you. I won't let them break you. I WILL find you."

Her hand drifted to the sketchbook left open on the desk. She traced the page lightly, eyes settling on the drawing within. Her likeness stared back at her, rendered in golden charcoal, her eyes left deliberately blank, empty spaces where she had always warned him not to define her.

"You never did draw me correctly," she sighed, smiling.

A whisper of darkness curled through the room and Eira straightened, senses snapping into focus as something moved behind her. This presence was not mortal, nor was it the familiar pulse of Balance asserting itself. Darkness brushed the back of her neck, cold and deliberate.

She flexed her fingers, calling her essence forward. Gold ignited in her eyes as power rolled off her in slow, controlled waves.

"Come out," she said, voice low. "You dare disturb this place? Show me who you are."

A figure emerged from the shadows, tall and unnaturally still, as though sunlight had never known him. He was neither Sovereign nor mortal. Eira felt the truth settle into her bones before her mind caught up. A herald of The Fates.

His skin was milky white, stretched smooth and unblemished, more like carved stone than flesh. His head was completely bare, scalp seamless and pale, giving him the unfinished look of something sculpted rather than born. His eyes were the same pallid shade, pupil-less and opaque, reflecting nothing, as if sight itself had been stripped from them. They did not blink nor wander. They simply *watched*.

Pewter robes draped his narrow frame, their color stark against the lifeless pallor of his skin. The fabric clung to him unnaturally, as though grown rather than worn, embroidered with faint silver sigils that pulsed softly in time with The Loom itself.

He did not breathe, because he did not need to. He stood as an extension of The Fates' will—an emissary shaped for obedience, as a messenger.

"Peace," he said, his voice multi-layered and snake-like. *"You should not be here."*

Eira stepped in front of Adrian's desk, shielding the memory of him from its cold stare. "Then you should not have taken him."

Her voice was calm. Power gathered beneath her skin, her essence flaring into a blinding white radiance that bled into the room. The air bent around her, pressure mounting as she lifted her gaze fully to the herald. "Would you like to try to remove me?"

The herald tilted his head. *"Your realm resists you. Your essence is ... different. You are becoming something that cannot exist. Surely you know that your time is coming."*

Eira's eyes flared gold, the last traces of green burning away. When she spoke, her voice slipped into a lower register, layered and resonant, carrying an inflection that did not belong to Peace.

She smiled. "Then take me."

The herald did not move, only stared at her. *"The more you fight, the more you feed what grows inside you, Sovereign of Peace."*

Eira stepped forward, voice shaking with untamed fury. "Tell me where he is or leave this place."

"That, I cannot do," he hissed, *"though you should know, you will answer for all of your transgressions soon enough."*

Eira did not raise her voice at the herald; she did not need to. She could eviscerate him with a mere thought, but obliterating The Fates' messenger would be in poor taste. For now.

"You will tell me," she said softly, "or I will extract the truth from someone who survives longer."

The herald paused, and silence filled the space between them. He almost seemed ... afraid. Her eyes never left him as she watched him take a few careful steps back, the faint glow of the threads woven through his form dimming as if they were retreating into themselves. The air around him tightened, drawn thin by the weight of her attention. For a being meant to stand before Sovereigns without flinching, his resolve was cracking at the edges.

Eira frowned in annoyance, the expression subtle but sharp—an imperfection in her composure that carried more threat than rage ever could. Fear was inconvenient. Hesitation even more so.

"Do not mistake my patience for mercy," she said coolly. "If you are going to retreat, do so with purpose. Otherwise, speak."

"Something stirs in you," he said in a low, raspy voice. *"Something that should not exist in your form. You are warned to be still, Sovereign of Peace."*

Eira's pulse roared in her ears as the room filled with brilliant light. She had no use for his riddles, and even less tolerance for his continued presence. The herald recoiled as she stepped closer, predatory now, her calm tightening into something lethal. "Where is Adrian? Where are *they* keeping him?"

She was done listening to him talk. Words had lost their usefulness the moment he chose warnings over truth. She had given him space—time enough to decide whether he would speak as a messenger or cower like a witness afraid of his own knowledge. That patience thinned now, drawn to a razor's edge.

She wanted answers, and she would take them. Violently. The calm around her did not shatter. It *compressed*. The world seem to fold inward, sound dulling as if the world itself had been wrapped in layers of quiet. The threads anchoring the herald to The Loom screamed in silent protest, flaring once before dimming to a panicked, erratic glow. Eira felt the shape of him—not his body, but the pattern of him

—every tether, every safeguard placed to keep Sovereigns from doing exactly this.

She stepped forward and distance vanished. Her presence closed around him, not as force, but as inevitability. The kind of pressure that made resistance pointless because it did not seek permission.

The herald took one step back as his voice trembled. *"He is in the temple of The Three. But YOU are not welcome there."*

With that, the herald dissolved into ash and shadow, his final words hanging in the air. *"If you seek to free him ... you will bring war upon all creation."*

Eira closed her eyes, exhaling a slow, deliberate breath. "Then war it is."

CHAPTER 7
EIRA

Sleep had not come easily to Eira for a long while. When it did come, it never arrived gently. It took her without warning, pulling her down through layers of consciousness until the world dissolved into darkness that fractured, blurring thought into memory, then into nothingness.

Tonight, that darkness refused to remain empty. It bent and folded around her, threads of gold and shadow weaving together until the sensation settled into something unmistakable. It felt like a presence, a heartbeat she recognized as instinctively as her own.

"Eira." Adrian's voice cut through the dream, clear but unsteady, like sunlight breaking through heavy cloud.

She turned toward him instinctively, her pulse racing

as her body recognized him before her mind dared to believe he was there.

He stood several paces away in a place that defied definition. It was not the mortal realm, nor The Loom. It existed between them all, a suspended space shaped by memory and longing, barely holding him there.

His eyes glowed softly, gold flickering beneath the surface like embers buried under ash. Faint bindings circled his wrists, translucent but unmistakable, marks exposing The Fate's hold on him. He looked worn in a way that went deeper than exhaustion, as though the weight of what he carried had settled into his bones.

The distance she felt from him arrived all at once, sharp enough to hurt. She recognized him anyway, and the familiarity stirred a quiet excitement beneath the ache. He was beautiful and he was here in this moment.

"Adrian," she whispered, stepping toward him in awe. "You are ... here? Tell me this is real."

His mouth curved into a careful, pained smile. "I am, at least for a little while. I had to see you."

She reached for him without thinking. Her hand lifted, fingers trembling as they hovered inches from his arm. At the last moment she drew back, heart pounding, as doubt surged through her.

Her slight recoil did not go unnoticed by him. "You're afraid of me," he said quietly, brow furrowing.

The words struck her harder than she expected. Eira

swallowed, her throat burning. "Afraid of you? No, I am angry with you, Adrian. You lied to me."

His jaw tightened, but his eyes softened. "I didn't lie Eira, I withheld the truth, and for good reason."

"Withholding truth is a lie," *she replied, sharper than she meant to be. Her voice faltered despite her effort to steady it.* "Why didn't you tell me what you were?"

Adrian looked away, drawing in a slow breath, as if the answer itself was too much to bear. "Because I was terrified that if you knew, you would run. I never want you to run from me ... or pull away, like you're doing now."

Anger flared hot and sudden within her. "I am the Sovereign of Peace," *she said.* "I do not run. Especially not from you. Not from the man I love."

He lifted his gaze to hers, and the heartbreak there nearly undid her. "You are becoming something far greater than Peace, Eira."

Her spine stiffened, her gaze narrowing on him. She did not want to be angry with the man she loved, but the sensation rising within her was unfamiliar—too sharp to ignore, too heavy to name; for her, at least.

"Is that why you hid it?" *she asked quietly, her head tilting to the side.* "Did you know this shift was a possibility?"

"No," *he said at once, stepping closer.* "I hid it because The Fates wanted me dead from the moment I was born. If they learned you knew, if they learned you loved me, they would have punished you to keep us apart."

Eira's breath caught painfully in her throat. "You should have trusted me with that knowledge."

"I do trust you, Eira," he said softly. "That's why I stayed. That's why I risked everything to be near you."

"But you did not trust me with knowledge," she replied quietly. "You could have told me what you were. A demigod, Adrian. How did I not sense it from you?"

Silence settled between them, heavy and unyielding. The dream space shimmered, threads tightening as though strained by their proximity. Adrian took another step closer, the air vibrating with restrained force.

"Eira," he said, his voice breaking, "I love you. If you don't believe anything else, please believe that. I love you with everything that I am, mortal and god alike."

The words struck her hard enough to steal her breath. She stepped back, shaking her head, her chest aching with the effort to inhale.

"I am so angry with you," she said, voice breaking on the last word. "You kept the truth from me. Me, Adrian!"

The anger that followed surprised her. It rose sharp and unbidden, out of place against the longing that still pulled her toward him. All she wanted was to be close to him in this moment, to take whatever time the dream allowed. Instead, something else pressed forward beneath the surface, insistent and restless, urging her toward fury she did not want.

She pushed it down. She did not know when she would see him again, or if this would be the last moment they were given. If this was all the time she had, she would not spend it consumed by anger.

His voice cracked. "I knew what I was. I knew that they wanted me. Eira, I didn't want you to carry that burden! I didn't want to become your enemy or your ruin."

"And yet here we are," she whispered, tears burning behind her eyes. "You, bound to The Loom; and me, unraveling because of it. By design, you are my enemy, Adrian."

Eira shook her head, jaw tightening as the air around her vibrated in response to her turmoil. "Why should we suffer for things beyond our control? Can I have love and not be punished for it?"

The space around them flickered violently, threads snapping and reforming as if the dream itself were struggling to endure. Adrian reached for her. He did not touch her, but the intent was there, powerful as any contact.

"I will find a way," he said, resolve hardening his tone. "A way for us to exist without destroying each other; without breaking the world."

"How?" she asked. "How do you break free when The Fates could use you as a weapon against me? Against my siblings? Your blood connection threatens my existence!"

"I don't know the answer to that question, Eira," he admitted. "But I will find a way. I will not be used against you. There is no one in this realm or the others that could turn me into a weapon against you."

Her voice dropped as she stared at his face, memorizing every beautifully sculpted feature. "You have become my weakness, Adrian. I feel myself wanting to rip the world apart. A Sovereign should not have a weakness."

His expression softened into something unbearably gentle as a smile tugged at his lips. "Well that's interesting, because you are my strength."

Tears slipped free despite her effort to hold them back. "This is why Sovereigns are not meant to feel such emotions. My heart—" Eira pointed to her heart, emphasizing her words, "feels like it is being ripped from my chest. And it doesn't cease. It never, ever relents. I wish it would, just for a moment. I need a moment of peace from this unrest."

"I know," he said quietly. "I know, love. I wish I could make this right. There are so many things I wish I could have done differently. But I will find a way to you. I will always be yours, Eira. My heart will always belong to you, and you alone."

When she glanced up at him, he was closer than before. Close enough that their foreheads nearly touched, light sparking between them.

"Eira," he murmured, staring at her intently, longingly.

"Yes?" she whispered, holding on to the faint echo of his heartbeat as she gazed into his dark eyes, then trailing down to his lips. She wished she could kiss them once more.

"You're changing," he said. "I can feel it through the threads."

She flinched at this, surprised that he could feel it. "You can?"

"Yes, I can. Stop fighting it," *he continued.* "I think ... I think who you're becoming is powerful enough to break them."

She stilled, her gaze searching his. "You don't know that, Adrian. I don't even know that."

Adrian's smile softened. "I know you. You are a Sovereign, no matter what form that takes."

Her voice trembled. "I don't know myself anymore. It is becoming more difficult to recognize myself each day."

"You will," *he said, his voice steady with a confidence she did not share.* "And when you do, you will come for me."

Her eyes roamed his face before locking onto his. She didn't dare tear them away. "Adrian ... " *she whispered, reaching for him.*

For a moment, his face contorted, as if something inside him ached to break free. Then his eyes softened as he looked at her the way he had in the beginning—with awe, with wonder, with a devotion that bordered on worship.

"You truly are the most beautiful woman I have ever seen," *he said softly, reverently, as a faint smile tugged at the corner of his mouth.* "I would kneel before you, Eira."

His hand lifted toward her, then stilled, fingers curling into a fist as he realized that more than distance held him back. Tears welled visibly in Eira's eyes as she watched him, her eyes tracking his motion.

"My heart," he murmured, clutching at his chest. *"You're here. You're always here."* As if to steady himself, he placed his other hand over it, pressing gently, grounding the feeling before it consumed him.

The weight of his words sank into her heart, burrowing deep until they crowded out every other thought, leaving only the space where he existed. Her fingers hovered inches from his hand, close enough to feel the heat of him and the pull of something ancient and dangerous. Her mouth parted as she gasped. "Adrian—"

The dream fractured around them, threads snapping apart like brittle branches. As Adrian faded, his voice reached her one last time.

"I love you. And nothing The Fates do will erase that."

Then he was gone.

Eira jolted upright, breath tearing from her as if she had surfaced from deep water. The echo of him still clung to her skin. She could feel the weight of his presence and the certainty of his love. She folded back into the field of blossoms where she had collapsed, longing settling so deep within her it bordered on pain. The dream had torn open every wound she had tried to seal. He loved her. He had lied to her. Both truths existed together, and the contradiction cut deeper than either one alone.

Above her, the sky pulsed faintly, threads of light weaving behind the clouds like veins beneath skin. She lifted her hand toward the sky, closing her eyes.

"Adrian."

His name carried too many meanings at once. Memory. Promise. Betrayal.

She pressed her palms to her eyes, breathing through the ache. "How can you love me, and I you," she whispered, "when your existence could undo everything I am?"

How could she still want him? How could she long for him when he carried the potential to become her enemy? A tear slid into the flowers beside her like silver dew.

"I don't know how to save you without losing myself," she said. "I don't know how to be Peace when all I feel is ruin."

The threads above her shuddered in response. The field rippled as something deep beneath the world shifted, heavy with anticipation.

Eira sat up sharply. The sensation reached her all at once, vast and unmistakable, pressing against her awareness with a weight she had never felt before. It was older than the Sovereigns themselves, not reaching for her so much as asserting its presence.

Understanding settled slowly, cold and certain. Whatever was coming was not waiting for her to decide. The world was already responding, and it was warning her to make her choice.

CHAPTER 8
EIRA

Eira sat among the pale blue blossoms of her realm, the ground cool beneath her palms. The field was quiet, bordered by clear water that reflected the low, bluish-grey sky. Willow branches swayed faintly at the edges of the meadow, their leaves brushing the surface of the water with soft, repetitive whispers.

This place had once steadied her. It had been her sanctuary when the demands of her duty grew too loud. Now, even here, she felt the strain and knew that her time of judgement was coming. Perhaps sooner than later.

Threads of gold traced faint paths through the sky above her, woven so thoroughly into cloud and air that she could not tell where one ended and the other began. Once, their presence had meant stability and harmony. Now they felt like reminder and resolve all at once.

Eira closed her eyes and drew in a slow breath, allowing the weight of everything she carried to settle fully. She did not fight the memory when it surfaced. She had avoided it long enough. The memory pressed in on her, even now.

THE RUINS RETURNED to her with unsettling clarity. Eira remembered the cold stone beneath her bare feet and the way mist had curled through the broken pillars of the ruins, dampening the hem of her gown. The hall had been vast and silent, as though the place itself had been forgotten by time. Inscriptions lined the floor and walls, worn but deliberate, pulling at her attention with a persistence she had not understood at the time.

Her gaze had been drawn to the carving almost immediately. A mortal figure, etched carefully into the stone, with threads wound between his fingers. She had traced them that night until her skin burned, and she could still feel the grooves long after she stepped away.

She did not know it at the time, but that carving was perhaps a prophecy of what was to come. A warning that the Sovereigns were meant to heed.

She remembered wondering why Adrian had to be the mortal to see the threads, and what the implications of that could mean.

Then The Watcher had emerged from the shadows, his presence quiet but unmistakable. He had not carried the weight of a Sovereign, nor the fragility of a mortal. His face had been marked by centuries rather than age, his pale eyes sharp with awareness rather than distance.

"You will not find the answer by staring at stone," he had said.

"Adrian sees the threads," she had whispered to him. "He draws them. He dreams about them. It cannot be by chance."

She remembered the flicker of hope and dread that had followed.

"It is not by chance," The Watcher had said. "The Seers were born rarely, once in many generations."

But The Watcher had been wrong—so very wrong—or perhaps he had known a truth that had not been meant for her at the time.

"He is something else entirely," The Watcher had said. "Cursed, perhaps."

She remembered her refusal, the way she had defended Adrian without hesitation, insisting that his gentleness mattered more than any gift he carried. The Watcher had not argued. He had only warned her.

AT THE TIME, Eira had heard caution. She had not heard inevitability. Sitting in her field now, Eira understood the difference. She opened her eyes to the present, to the threads above her, noticing the way they pressed against her awareness without moving or tightening. She now realized that The Watcher had not been warning her away from Adrian. He had been preparing her for what loving him would cost.

She exhaled slowly, her chest aching with a rawness she could no longer dismiss. She now knew there was one being who had seen this path clearly from the beginning. The Watcher had been erased from history, but not from the world. He had endured because he understood what The Loom would not acknowledge—not to The Architect nor the Sovereigns.

Eira rose to her feet and brushed the petals from her white gown, steadying herself as her breathing slowed and a sense of calm returned. She reached outward with her essence, letting it stretch toward the distant ruins she could not see but knew as surely as her own breath.

"It is time," she said softly, no longer to remember or wonder, but to ask the question she had avoided for far too long.

CHAPTER 9
EIRA

The veil to the lost realm resisted her. Eira felt it the moment her palm met the thinning air, a subtle but distinct resistance, like pressure held just shy of pain. The space before her shimmered faintly, and reality stretched taut enough to hum beneath her touch. Threads tightened around the point of contact, their low vibration carrying a warning she had learned to recognize long ago.

Once, she would have withdrawn and let caution guide her, allowing peace to settle the disturbance before it could become something worse. She would have listened to the quiet insistence of The Loom and stepped back into Balance without question. That instinct did not come now, and her blind loyalty to The Loom had neared its end.

Eira drew a slow breath and let her attention shift

inward, toward the anger she had been holding at a careful distance. It rose readily, not wild but contained; a force shaped by grief and unanswered questions. When she pressed her hand forward again, the resistance gave way. The veil tore soundlessly as she stepped through, and Eira felt a flicker of grim satisfaction at the knowledge that she would not be asking for permission again.

The air on the other side felt cold and heavy, no doubt by age rather than chill. It tasted of stone and secrecy, a place held in time rather than a place meant to entertain visitors. The space beyond did not welcome nor reject her. It simply existed, indifferent to her presence in a way that felt deliberate. The Sovereigns had always known of the ruins, though they never had much cause to visit this realm. Until now.

There was no sky in the way mortals would understand it. Above her stretched a vast expanse of bluish-grey haze, neither dawn nor dusk. The ground beneath her feet was smooth, dark stone, echoing faintly with each step. She moved forward carefully, aware of the way the air resisted motion here, not physically but conceptually, as though the realm itself had grown unused to being crossed.

Eira walked through the ruins, noting the way the massive columns stretched upward into shadow, their upper halves fractured or missing entirely, leaving the space above them open and unresolved. A thin mist lingered near the ground, gathering and dispersing, brushing against her ankles as she walked. This place remained exactly the same as the last time she had visited, as she knew it always would.

The place felt unchanged in its structure, but not in its presence. Something about it had shifted, subtle enough that she might have missed it if she had not been paying attention. The air felt alert, as though the hall itself had noticed her return, or been waiting for it.

"This feels different," she murmured to herself, taking in the space around her.

She stopped beneath one of the pillars and looked up. Threads moved overhead, faint but visible, stretched more tightly than she remembered. One in particular caught her attention, drawn thin as it spanned the open space above her. She reached for it, curiosity overriding caution.

The moment her essence closed around it, a sharp, immediate pain shot through her body, radiating outward from the intrusion. She gasped but did not release it. The thread vibrated violently, its tension increasing as though resisting her grip. It did not want to be held, but Eira refused to let it go. Eira tightened her hold, allowing this small act of rebellion.

One moment Eira held the thread with her essence, the next the thread snapped. Light burst outward in a silent wave, rippling through the hall with enough force to make the ground beneath her feet groan. The pillars shuddered, sending debris flying from their surfaces as if shaken loose from sleep. Eira stumbled back, instinctively raising her arm to shield herself as the broken thread disintegrated into fine gold dust that vanished before it could settle.

The resistance should have been enough to warn her, but it was not. She decided that she would no longer listen to warnings. She would reach for truth herself. She waited, expecting reprisal, or some immediate correction from The Loom. Instead, the hall grew still and the air seemed to ease, tension draining from it as if the space itself had been waiting for that exact moment.

Eira lowered her arm slowly, her heart pounding wildly. A small grin tugged at the corner of her mouth and she felt an odd sense of satisfaction. Nothing happened. She pressed a hand to her chest, feeling her pulse race beneath her skin. Something stirred there, unfamiliar and restless, not fear but a sharpened awareness that beckoned for her to awaken it.

"What am I becoming," she whispered, the question escaping her lips before she could stop it.

The ruins offered no answer, but they were not empty. A faint hum lingered in the air, subtle and persistent, tugging at her attention. She followed it deeper into the hall, her steps measured now, alert to every shift in sound and sensation. She expected The Watcher to appear at any moment, but he did not.

Her hand brushed against one of the carved pillars as she paused, fingers tracing grooves worn deep into the stone. She knew this carving. She had memorized it once without realizing she was doing so. The figure etched into the wall stared back at her, unchanged. She had traced its shape before until her skin burned, driven by a need she had not been able to name.

"Adrian," she breathed, closing her eyes as she thought of him. She would not—could not—allow her mind to wander at this moment. She had come to the ruins for answers, not to linger on a memory.

Something moved at the far end of the hall, a subtle shift of shadow that resolved into form as it approached. Recognition settled in.

"I know you are here," she said, voice steady as she turned to face the presence fully. "Watcher."

He emerged from the edge of the ruins, his tattered robe caught between light and dark, as though neither fully claimed him.

"So Peace returns," he said, voice low and measured as he looked her over. "But you are not the same."

"No," Eira replied with a sly smile, "I am not."

The Watcher's gaze flicked briefly upward, toward the tightened threads overhead. "They feel you now.

The Fates are aware of what stirs in you, and the world did not end," he observed.

"No," Eira said, looking beyond him now, "it did not. Not yet."

"Then you begin to understand why they fear you." His words landed heavily, no doubt the effect he wanted them to have on Eira.

Eira swallowed and forced her focus steady. "I need answers, Watcher."

"Then ask," he said, waving his hand toward the ruins.

She did not hesitate this time. "How do I rewrite what has already been written?"

The air shifted, wind stirring for the first time since she entered the realm. Dust lifted from the floor, inscriptions along the pillars glowing faintly as something stirred.

"That," The Watcher said slowly, as if measuring his words, "is a complicated question with many answers."

Understanding settled into her with chilling clarity. Relief and terror still lived, but neither ruled her. She met The Watcher's gaze without flinching, already grasping the truth he was circling.

"To answer simply, yes," he said at last. "But only by one who stands beyond their reach by becoming an entity that is other than the order they know."

His eyes locked onto hers as he inclined his head in

recognition. Eira did not look away. She understood him instantly, and did not shy away from the truth of it. Whatever fear lingered was sealed deep inside her, contained. If that was what it required, then she would become unreachable.

Her pulse was steady when she spoke. "And that is me."

The Watcher offered no reply, because none was needed. His gaze remained fixed on hers, unwavering, and the quiet that stretched between them carried its own confirmation—one no denial could undo.

Eira straightened, resolve settling into place not as certainty, but as commitment. "Then tell me what I have to do," she said.

The Watcher lifted his hand, and the ruins shifted around them, stone bending with the slow recognition of something ancient roused from forgetfulness.

"Listen carefully," he said. "Because the truth you seek will change everything you believe to be true."

CHAPTER 10
EIRA

The Watcher's hand remained raised as the ruins completed their slow, deliberate shift. Lines etched into the broken pillars brightened from within, not with light but with awareness, as if the hall itself were waking after a long and unwilling sleep. The air thickened, vibrating faintly, and the threads overhead drew taut until they hummed beneath Eira's skin.

She felt it before she saw it. The ruins were no longer a place. It was a threshold to somewhere else entirely. Eira's breath caught as the floor beneath her feet seemed to deepen, layers of stone unfolding into one another, revealing shapes and patterns that did not exist a moment before. Symbols slid along the walls, rearranging themselves with quiet precision, responding not to The Watcher's command alone, but to her presence.

"This is not memory as mortals understand it," The Watcher said calmly. His voice carried differently now, resonating through the stone rather than the air. "What you are about to see is a truth that was never meant to be known."

Eira nodded once in acknowledgment, a soft gold light stirring behind her eyes as her essence answered the change in the realm. "Even The Architect has secrets, then," she said, certainty settling into her tone.

"Yes," he said, lowering his hand as the world tilted around them.

The shift carried the sensation of being drawn inward. The ruined hall dimmed at the edges of her vision as the stone beneath her feet warmed, pulsing faintly. She realized then that the ruins were not showing her the past. They were allowing her to stand inside it.

Shadows lengthened, stretching into shapes that moved with purpose. Threads emerged from the stone itself, faint and translucent, weaving through the air like ghostly veins. Eira recognized them instantly. These were not from The Loom as it existed now, but its earliest patterns, raw and powerful.

"This is from the beginning," she said quietly.

"It is," The Watcher replied. "The beginning, and what happened after."

Images surfaced within the stone—vast forms moving through an endless expanse; Titans, immense and eternal, shaping reality through presence alone. Their essence was brilliant and volatile, power without restraint.

"The old gods ... the Titans," Eira whispered, more to herself than The Watcher.

"They were born of raw power," The Watcher said. "Creation without restraint. Creation like that cannot last." His gaze lingered on the shifting vision. "The Architect made certain of it."

Eira watched as the vision shifted. Large creatures emerged, terrifying luminous things born into the wake of that immense power. They clustered instinctively toward the Titans, drawn by the gravity of creation itself. She felt their wonder first, then their fear.

Worlds ignited around the creatures, beautiful and expansive. Galaxies bloomed in violent bursts of light, spiraling outward like sparks from a struck blade. For a heartbeat, the creations burned with promise.

Then the Titans turned upon them, unleashing their destructive nature. Stars were torn apart midbirth. Worlds were swallowed before they could cool, before life could take root. The Titans consumed without restraint, stripping creation down to its final resonance until even light itself seemed to scream as it was devoured. Entire systems vanished into their grasp, erased without resistance. The light was torn apart, collapsing back into darkness. What had been born moments before was unmade just as quickly, erased without memory or mourning.

To Eira, it passed in the span of a single breath—a flicker of devastation too vast for the mind to fully grasp. Yet she knew the truth beneath the illusion. This destruction did not end quickly. It stretched across ages, unchecked, repeating itself until something powerful enough finally rose to stop it.

Eira's jaw tightened as the stone darkened. "And this is where he intervened."

"Yes," The Watcher replied. His voice remained steady, but the sadness beneath it was evident to her.

A new presence entered the vision. It had no form, no face, no single point the eye could fix upon. It arrived as pressure—an intelligence so vast it bent the chaos around it simply by existing. It did not belong to the destruction it moved through, and the chaos recoiled from it instinctively.

"The Architect," she said.

"He did not destroy them," The Watcher continued, his voice low and measured. "Not entirely. He divided them. What could be governed, he bound. What could not, he cast into containment."

The vision fractured and figures were pulled away, unraveling into the depths of a vast, silent chasm.

Others were sealed beyond reach, their echoes piercing until silence fell.

The Watcher lowered his hand slightly, though the vision held.

"We thought they were unmade," she said, her voice steady but threaded with something sharper. "That nothing of them remained. I did not know that they were ... contained."

The ruins hummed, responding to the proof of her understanding.

She turned to face him fully. "If there is more, tell me."

The Watcher did not answer immediately. His silence stretched, deliberate and heavy. "The old gods were not destroyed," he said at last. "They were removed from the pattern. Severed from continuity and existence. That is not the same thing as ending, and it is what Balance required."

Eira's eyes widened. "Then they still exist."

"In fragments," he replied. "In places most cannot reach."

Her fingers curled slowly at her side. "And if something exists ... "

The Watcher's pale eyes met hers. "It can be remembered," he said.

The implication settled between them, vast and terrifying.

"Or brought back," Eira finished. "And Adrian?" she asked, though she already felt the answer forming.

The vision shifted again and she watched as bloodlines unfolded. Threads weaving through generations, carrying fragments too subtle for The Loom to police. A spark, dormant and waiting, passed quietly from one life to the next until it found a vessel strong enough to hold it. It did not seek dominion, but endurance.

She felt the pattern take shape. The Titans had not been the only beings to rise in that first age. When their fall fractured creation, other gods emerged in the wake of that violence. Lesser, yes—but not insignificant. They carried echoes of the Titans within them, traces of that raw, formative power reshaped into something narrower, more stable. Sight. Flame. Song. Storm. Domains carved not from chaos, but from what remained after it was broken.

These gods were born of aftermath, not origin. Their time came and went. Some faded, while others were absorbed into myth. Some were folded quietly into The Architect's new order, allowed to exist so long as they did not remember too much of what had come before. Their bloodlines persisted even as their names dimmed, thinning with each generation, losing potency but never vanishing entirely. Power, Eira understood, was not so easily erased.

When the vision passed, The Watcher turned

toward one of the fractured pillars, brushing his fingertips along the worn inscriptions carved deep into the surface. Dust lifted and drifted away at his touch, as though the ruin itself were exhaling, relieved to be seen.

"You know who his mother was, and her lineage." The Watcher said, and it was not a question.

"Yes," Eira said, nodding slowly as the threads aligned. "A daughter of Apollo."

Apollo's lineage flared faintly within the vision, not as a Sovereign, nor Titan, but something that had stood dangerously close to both. Sight that pierced veils and song that shaped memory.

"Apollo was permitted proximity," The Watcher said, "because he was not like his kin. Sight, in that lineage, had never been limited to vision alone. It was awareness and understanding. "

"And that proximity left residue," Eira said quietly.

She drew a steady breath, her voice calm despite the storm rising beneath it. Her hands trembled, and she curled them into fists to steady them. "So Adrian carries Apollo's blood, and something older beneath it."

The Watcher inclined his head. "Yes. Adrian carries an ember—one that still bears traces of the old gods. And he is not the only one. When the old gods were cast into The Chasm, they did not go whole. They fractured themselves. Their essence scattered outward in embers, sent into the world before containment closed around them."

"These embers settled into mortal inheritance," he continued, "passed quietly from one generation to the next. Separated, they are harmless—barely detectable."

He met her gaze. "But together," he said, voice lowering, "they could call back what was meant to remain contained."

Understanding struck Eira with brutal clarity.

"The Architect knows," she said. "That is why he keeps Adrian, allowing him to live."

"Yes," The Watcher replied, "for now. Binding is quieter than erasure. The Architect sealed realms, not inheritance. Blood moves beyond the reach of walls."

Her chest tightened painfully as the truth settled in place. "So Adrian isn't dangerous because of what he's done."

"No," The Watcher agreed.

"He's dangerous because of what he could become ... and because of me," she said, the realization cutting clean and deep.

The Watcher met her gaze steadily. "Proximity accelerates awakening. And love that was never meant to exist destabilizes containment."

"And me breaking our Law, disrupting Balance by falling in love with him could be the very thing that unleashes what was never meant to exist." Eira said quietly.

She drew a breath, steadying herself as understanding took hold. "But Adrian isn't bound because he is corrupted. He's bound because he exists between what can be governed and what cannot."

Her gaze lifted, sharp with clarity now. "If I remain what I am—contained and predictable—I can never reach him without destroying him or fracturing Balance. But if I transform," she continued, her voice lowering, "if I become something my nature was never meant to hold ... then I stand where he stands. Beyond the reach of The Loom's rules. Beyond the bindings of The Fates."

She met The Watcher's eyes. "Like Adrian, I would no longer belong entirely to Balance. And from there, I can save him."

The Watcher did not correct her, and that silence told her everything.

EIRA DID NOT RETURN to the ruins after The Watcher finished speaking. She left without ceremony, stepping back through the thinning veil while the ancient hall settled into itself again. The transition was seamless in the way all things governed by The Loom were meant to be. One moment the air was heavy with age and old truths, the next it opened into the familiar quiet of her realm.

She stood at the edge of the field, pale blossoms bending gently around her ankles, clear water stretching outward in calm reflection. Willow branches swayed above the surface, their leaves whispering against one another in a rhythm she had known for centuries.

Eira took a slow step forward and then another, waiting for the sense of alignment that usually followed her return. Normally, the field welcomed her, adjusting without effort. Peace did not impose itself here. It *belonged*. Now, the stillness hesitated.

It was so subtle, she might have missed it if she had not been paying attention. The threads woven through the air lagged behind her movements, their glint delayed by the smallest fraction of a moment. When she lifted her hand, the field did not immediately respond. The flowers bent, but not quite in time with her breath.

Eira lowered her arm slowly. "You are imagining it," she murmured, though the words carried little conviction.

She crossed the field toward the water's edge, the hem of her gown brushing petals that should have felt like home. Instead, the sensation slid past her awareness without settling. When she knelt and pressed her fingers into the cool surface of the water, the reflection wavered strangely, recoiling from her touch.

Eira withdrew her hand and closed her eyes, forcing herself to breathe evenly. The Watcher's voice lingered in her thoughts:

Binding is quieter than erasure.

She had always known The Loom corrected imbalances. She had believed that meant restoration. Now she understood it also meant containment.

Eira opened her eyes and stared out across the water. Adrian's face surfaced unbidden in her mind, not as he had been bound, fearful and uncertain, but as he had been when he thought no one was watching. She remembered how often he hesitated before touching her, wondering if he was measuring; not desire but consequence. At the time, she had thought it was caution. Now she wondered if it had been restraint.

Eira pushed herself to her feet and turned away from the water. She needed movement, because stillness no longer helped. As she crossed deeper into her realm, she tested herself in small, deliberate ways. She reached toward a knot of threads tangled near the roots of a willow, intending to smooth them into alignment. Normally, the motion required little effort—Peace was not force, it was invitation. But the threads resisted. Not enough to provoke correction. Just enough to remind her they were no longer wholly compliant. Eira felt the tension snap lightly against her awareness, a quiet refusal that left her hand suspended in midair.

She withdrew, letting the threads settle on their own. The moment stretched longer than it should have before Balance reasserted itself. Eira stared at the space where her hand had been.

Proximity accelerates awakening.

She turned back toward the center of her realm, anger stirring beneath the surface of her calm. Not the sharp fury of defiance, but something colder and more focused. She had spent centuries ensuring Balance endured. She had never once questioned whether Balance itself could be afraid, but she questioned it now.

When she reached the sanctuary grove near the heart of her domain, she slowed. This place had always responded to her without hesitation. If something had shifted, she would feel it here. Eira stepped into the clearing and stilled. The threads overhead shimmered faintly, their pattern intact but altered in a way that left a lingering ache within her. The alignment was correct. The execution was not.

She reached for the threads again, more carefully this time, guiding rather than directing. The response came, but it felt distant, and that difference mattered. Eira exhaled slowly and lowered her hands. For the first time since she had been shaped into Peace, she understood that her role was no longer unquestioned. She was still a Sovereign, but she was no longer neutral.

A flicker of presence brushed the edge of her awareness, faint but unmistakable. She knew it was not The Watcher. Not The Fates. It was something closer.

Containment protocols adjusted.

Eira went very still. "Adjusted for whom," she asked the empty air.

No answer came, but she felt the direction of the correction immediately. Not toward her. Toward Adrian.

Eira exhaled sharply as she felt the shift ripple outward through the threads that connected realms; converging somewhere far from her sanctuary, tightening around a single point. The sensation was familiar enough to recognize, different enough to terrify her. They were reinforcing his bindings; not as punishment, but as precaution.

Eira's hands curled into fists. She had always believed The Loom corrected after harm was done. Now she understood what it had cost. But Adrian had not done anything wrong.

She turned sharply, scanning the grove as if the answer might be etched into the air. Her instincts urged her to intervene, to reroute the correction, to absorb the imbalance herself if that was what it took. Peace demanded restraint so Eira hesitated.

The Watcher's voice surfaced again, quieter this time. *"You did not cause this. You revealed it."*

She closed her eyes and pressed her palm against the center of her chest, steadying her breath. Intervention would draw attention. Direct interference would provoke a response she was not yet prepared to face. But doing nothing felt like betrayal, and that hurt as much as not being able to save Adrian.

Her gaze lifted to the threads overhead, tracing the path tightening somewhere beyond her reach. The Loom did not forbid her from acting because it expected her not to. That realization settled cold and heavy in her chest and it was then Eira made her choice.

CHAPTER II
EIRA

Eira did not expect the space where the threads converged to feel altered, yet the change was unmistakable the moment she crossed its threshold. The Loom lay thicker here, its paths layered so tightly that the air itself felt oppressive, as though possibility had been compressed into something almost solid. It was a place she had visited countless times in centuries past, always with the same quiet reverence, always with the same instinctive restraint. Today, restraint came more deliberately. It had to be chosen.

She stood still and allowed the space to acknowledge her on its own terms. The threads continued their motion, weaving and unweaving with precise indifference, but she could feel the subtle lag where her presence pressed against them. A hesitation, no more than that. Enough to tell her she was noticed.

It was not a summons. She had not called them. She had learned long ago that to summon was to concede authority, and she had not come to concede anything. The air cooled gradually, thinning until even her thoughts felt too loud. Awareness gathered around her in increments, not arriving but resolving, like a lens slowly adjusting into focus. When The Fates appeared, it was without spectacle—no surge of power, no announcement—only presence.

Solenne leaned against the nothingness beside her, silver hair loose and gleaming against the dim light of The Loom. Her posture was casual, almost languid, but her eyes were sharp with recognition rather than surprise. Virelith stood a short distance away, dark hair framing a face that revealed nothing. She watched Eira with measured attention, as though assessing a variable whose behavior had shifted outside expectation. Umbra occupied the space between them, golden hair catching the faint glow of the threads. She smiled as Eira looked up; a small, knowing curve of her mouth that carried neither warmth nor welcome.

The Three exchanged glances, a silent communication that felt deliberately exclusive, as though the conversation had already begun before Eira arrived.

Solenne broke the silence with a sigh. "It seems

you've been busy," she said, rolling her eyes as though tired of her own words. "'Why now?'" She waved a hand dismissively. "Haven't you caused enough trouble, little dove?"

"Too much, sister," Virelith said, her voice even.

Umbra's gaze remained fixed on Eira. "Another problem to fix," she said, almost thoughtfully, "if Peace so chooses this path."

The words struck with precision. Eira felt the familiar tightening in her chest, the reflexive urge to step back into composure, into silence. She resisted it, fingers curled slowly at her sides, nails pressing into her palms, anchoring her in the present moment.

"What business do you have with me?" she asked. Her voice did not rise, but the threads overhead shifted faintly all the same.

Umbra laughed softly. "Careful," she said. "The Loom is still displeased by you, fiery one."

"I do not intend to charm you," Eira replied, sneering.

Solenne's brows lifted, interest sharpening. "No," she said, "but you will heed our warning."

"Nothing good ever comes of that," Eira said, eyes glowing.

Virelith's eyes flicked briefly to the threads above them, then returned to Eira. "Change sometimes requires intervention, Sovereign."

"Ah," Eira replied. "Does it? Have you three not intervened enough, sisters?"

Umbra's smile thinned. "You speak as though something has been taken from you."

Eira met her gaze steadily. "I speak of *someone* you have taken from me."

The air tightened, pressure gathering without force. The Loom hummed, attentive.

Solenne straightened slightly. "You are treading close to accusation, little dove."

"I am acknowledging truth," Eira stated defiantly, "nothing more."

Virelith stepped forward a fraction. "Your concern lies outside your domain."

"Peace has never existed with such conflict," Eira said, "and as you know, stability does not maintain itself."

Umbra studied her with open calculation. "And yet stability has been maintained."

"For now," Eira replied.

The silence that followed was deliberate. The threads overhead shifted, narrowing by imperceptible degrees. Eira felt it along her spine, a tightening that had nothing to do with fear.

"You are advised to disengage," Virelith said.

Eira did not answer immediately. She looked instead at the threads; the endless intersections of choice and consequence, the paths that narrowed and expanded with each unseen decision.

"I will decide for myself this time, sisters," she said, narrowing her eyes.

Solenne laughed, sharp and humorless. "That's a dangerous choice."

"So is preemptive correction," Eira replied.

Umbra stepped closer, her presence warming the space even as it sharpened it. "Attachment compromises clarity."

"My clarity has never been the issue," Eira said defiantly.

"Attachment destabilizes," Umbra continued quietly.

"So does fear," Eira replied.

The Loom shuddered, threads tightening briefly before settling again. Eira felt the shift resonate through her, not as pain, but as pressure—like standing too close to something meant to be restrained.

"You are exceeding your design," Virelith said.

"Am I," Eira replied, coldly.

The words were simple, unadorned. They did not need emphasis. The space responded anyway, awareness pressing closer, heavier, as though measuring the cost of her presence.

"You would do well to remember your nature,"

Umbra said. "It is the only protection you will be afforded."

Eira inclined her head slightly, neither submissive nor defiant. "Peace has never meant obedience."

For a long moment, none of them spoke. Solenne's expression shifted from amusement to disdain. Virelith watched Eira with new attention, calculation replacing dismissal and Umbra's smile faded entirely.

"Do not mistake patience for permission," Umbra said as their forms began to recede.

Eira remained where she was until the space thinned again, until sound returned and the threads resumed their steady motion. Only then did she release the breath she had been holding. They had not forbidden nor denied her. But they had clearly warned her.

Eira turned away from the space, her steps slow and deliberate. She could still feel The Loom's awareness lingering; not hostile, not permissive, simply alert.

Something had shifted. Not in the threads, but in herself. She was no longer content to preserve Balance without question. She would no longer accept silence as virtue simply because it had once been her role. Whatever reckoning they believed awaited her, she would meet it standing.

And when the time came, she would not ask why. She would do what needed to be done.

CHAPTER 12
EIRA

Eira did not move for a long time after The Fates withdrew. The space they had occupied thinned slowly, awareness receding in reluctant layers until The Loom resumed its familiar hum and she was in her realm once more. But even now, her realm did not settle. The lake before her remained fractured, its surface split into uneven planes that reflected the sky at different angles, as if reality itself had failed to agree on what it was meant to show.

She stood at the edge of the water, her breathing shallow as she attempted to still the tremor running through her body. It did not stop, only intensified. Her hands shook when she lifted them into her line of sight. Not violently nor uncontrollably, but with a persistent vibration that seemed to come from beneath the skin. The sensation was unfamiliar and deeply unsettling, causing her essence to stir in resistance. Peace had always manifested as the absence of noise and excess. But this—this felt like accumulation, like something gathering momentum.

Eira clenched her fingers and then released them, but the tremor lingered all the same. It was sharp and narrowing, a sensation that pulled inward and asked to be released. It felt like a pressure that built instead of constricting.

Heat stirred beneath her skin, restless and unsettled, moving in a rhythm that did not belong to her. It shifted without her consent, coiling and uncoiling as though it had its own intent, a presence that refused to remain quiet no matter how tightly she tried to hold herself together. It felt old in a way that had nothing to do with age, buried so deeply it had nearly passed for absence. And yet it was there. Not fear. Not doubt. It was something ancient ... something that did not belong to Peace.

Eira exhaled sharply and dropped to her knees at the water's edge. The earth beneath her palms was cold, grounding in a way she desperately needed. The lake's fractured surface held still as she leaned closer, her reflection staring back at her without distortion or ripple as if her realm was afraid to move.

She closed her eyes and bent forward, forcing herself to breathe evenly. She had steadied worlds before, and knew she could steady herself. But when she reached inward, seeking the familiar calm she had always carried so effortlessly, she found resistance instead. And it was loud. It roared within her as though something was actively pushing back against containment.

Her breath hitched. She lifted her head and looked skyward, following the threads as they stretched overhead. They were closer than they had ever been, dense and watchful, their faint glow pulsing in measured response to her attention.

Once, she would have approached them with care, guided by the hard-earned restraint of someone who understood exactly what overreach could cost. That instinct no longer held. Eira sent her essence upward without hesitation nor deference, driving it into the threads with a force shaped by frustration and resolve, refusing to soften the contact or temper the intent behind it.

The response came at once.

The threads recoiled violently, snapping back as though burned, and the air cracked with the sound of sudden displacement as pressure slammed outward in a concussive wave that staggered her. The recoil lashed along her arms and spine, sharp and stinging, before a distant ripple of alarm raced through The Loom itself. Eira smiled as her hair lifted around her and the air began to heat.

Good. Let them feel it.

She pushed again, harder, and this time there was no restraint at all. Her essence tore upward and spilled through her realm like molten metal, dense and unyielding, warping everything it touched as the threads screamed and cinched tight around it. The force of it drove her backward, tearing the breath from her lungs as she fell onto the ground. Pain flared along her shoulders and down her back, but she barely registered it. She braced herself on one elbow and shoved upward again, refusing to retreat, refusing to yield.

"You will not deny me," she whispered, her voice rough and shaking as she gritted her teeth. "You will not decide what I am allowed to be. You will not resist me, the Sovereign of Peace. You will yield to ME."

Something answered.

It stirred deep in her chest, as though waking from a long and patient sleep. Heat unfurled beneath her ribs, spreading outward in widening arcs that pressed against her lungs and climbed her throat. Her vision blurred as gold bled into the edges of her sight. Eira gasped and seized the threads again, gripping them with fury she no longer bothered to contain. This time, they did not recoil—they fractured.

The light did not bloom—it detonated, ripping outward through her realm with a force that sent the lake surging in on itself, water rising in violent spirals before crashing back down. Trees bent under the impact, branches groaning as though the land itself were bracing. Above, the sky erupted, seams of molten gold tearing through the clouds before sealing over again, leaving the air scorched in their wake.

Eira screamed—not in pain, but in release. It was as if her body had waited eons for this moment. The burning spread through her, down her arms and along her spine, coiling into the core of her being until it felt as though she were being pulled apart and forged anew in one beat of her heart. Her hair whipped around her face as the air surged, the auburn darkening at the roots before bleeding into a deep, violent red. Strands sparked faintly with gold, smoke threading through the ends as though they had brushed flame.

Her breath stuttered. When she opened her eyes, the familiar swirl of green and gold was gone; replaced by a solid, unbroken burn—pure gold, blazing and unblinking. Power surged beneath her feet, spiraling upward until the ground split beneath the force. Her white gown dissolved into ash, scattering on the wind before reforming into black silk that wrapped around her like living shadow. The fabric moved with sharp, fluid intent, trailing behind her as though carried on a phantom wind.

A weight settled atop her head and Eira lifted her hand slowly, her fingers brushing cool metal shaped into jagged perfection. The crown pulsed faintly, forged from the broken threads themselves, its power foreign and deeply familiar all at once. Her heart thundered, each beat sending another tremor through the realm.

This was not calm. This was not Balance. This was not Peace.

Eira rose to her feet, the shadows of her gown curling around her ankles like smoke. Every nerve in her body hummed with energy, alive in a way she had never known. Behind her, a storm gathered of red, gold, and black; churning violently above the lake. Water rose in twisting columns, forming patterns that dissolved into flame before reforming again.

She knew that Peace could not hold a storm like this— but Chaos could. Her realm reacted instinctively. Trees leaned away from her presence, their branches darkening with sharp cracked foliage. The sky dimmed, streaks of crimson cutting through the grey like wounds that refused to close. Flowers withered beneath the wave of power, then bloomed again with twisted, obsidian petals that gleamed in the shifting light.

Eira watched the aftermath with a strange, unsettling satisfaction. She closed her eyes and breathed in the thrum of her new power, letting it sink deep into her bones. This was not what The Fates had wanted, nor what Peace had ever been allowed to become. It was not the shape The Architect had intended when he carved order from the wreckage of chaos. This was older than all of that—something the world had forgotten, buried so deeply that even existence itself had begun to believe it was gone.

Chaos did not ask permission. It did not kneel, nor did it wait.

Eira opened her eyes, gold blazing. "I am done begging," she said, her voice rolling outward, low and inexorable, like the first rumble of a coming storm.

The realm answered and in that moment, as the world shuddered beneath her feet, Eira understood with absolute clarity—if The Fates would not return Adrian, she would tear the world open until she reached him.

CHAPTER 13
THE LOOM
THE REALM REACTS

The Loom did not respond to Eira's change with caution. It reacted the way living things do when struck without warning. The disturbance tore through the weave in a single, violent surge; not spreading gradually but ripping outward in jagged lines that disrupted every thread it touched. Paths that had held steady for centuries shuddered and warped, their tension thrown abruptly off balance. Light flared and dimmed in erratic pulses, the golden expanse convulsing as though something fundamental had been struck from below.

The Loom had felt disruption before. War. Collapse. Extinction. But this was different. This was not an event moving through it ... this was something rising against it.

Across its vast and endless span, threads recoiled as if burned. Some snapped outright, severed so cleanly the space they had occupied screamed in their absence. Others writhed, tightening and loosening as though trying to remember what shape they were meant to hold.

A tremor rippled through every connected realm, a pressure that bent reality inward for a breath and then released it again. For a single, suspended moment, existence itself seemed to hesitate, recognizing that something that should have remained buried had awakened.

The Fates

Far from Eira's realm, The Fates felt the violent disruption. The light that filled their cavern surged sharply, its steady rhythm breaking as the weave convulsed. The pool at the chamber's center rippled violently, its surface shattering into overlapping reflections that refused to settle. The Fates stared at it in amusement that quickly turned to disapproval.

Solenne was the first to rise. Her usual languid posture snapped taut, silver hair lifting as though caught in a sudden current. Virelith's hand flew instinctively to the threads before her, fingers hovering just above their surface before flinching back as they recoiled from her touch. Umbra said nothing, but her expression had gone very still.

The threads before them twisted erratically, their glow brightening and dimming in rapid succession, as if struggling to stabilize around a disruption they could not contain.

"She has crossed something," Solenne said, her voice stripped of amusement.

"She has *entered* something," Virelith corrected, watching the weave with narrowed eyes.

Umbra stepped forward slowly, gaze fixed on the trembling Loom. "No," she said at last, with a sigh. "She has awakened it. What a shame."

The threads nearest Umbra's hand bled gold where her presence pressed too close, light seeping from them like a wound that refused to close.

"This was accounted for," Virelith said, though doubt edged her tone. "Delayed, perhaps, but contained. We knew this was a possibility. We can only push them but so far."

Solenne laughed once, sharp and brittle. "Contained?" She gestured at the weave, where fractures were already spreading. "Does that look contained to you?"

Umbra's eyes darkened. "We should have sealed her as soon as we felt the fracture."

"And still we allowed her proximity," Solenne

snapped. "Still we assumed Peace would remain what she was."

The pool at the chamber's center shuddered, its surface clearing abruptly as an image of Adrian appeared.

He was braced forward as if struck by an unseen force, breath dragging unevenly from his lungs. The bindings around his wrists shimmered violently, light flaring along their length as though something beneath them were pushing back.

Virelith's breath caught. "He feels it."

"He should not," Solenne said sharply. "The bindings—"

"—were never meant to hold against this," Umbra finished quietly.

In the image, Adrian's head lifted. Gold burned beneath his skin now, faint but visible; light threading through his veins like something waking after long confinement.

"He is reaching," Virelith whispered. "He is trying to reach her!"

Umbra's fingers curled slowly. "Find the threads she touched."

Solenne hesitated for the first time. "If we sever them—"

"—we may sever something that we alone cannot repair," Umbra said. "Yes."

The silence that followed was not reluctance, but calculation.

Death

Across the realms, the Sovereigns felt the disturbance not as knowledge, but as intrusion. Death felt it first. Thaloré had been crossing the threshold of his cathedral when the stone beneath his feet fractured with a sound like breaking ice. Souls recoiled in their currents, the rivers of passage hissing as their flow stuttered and surged. Pain lanced through him without warning, sharp and foreign. He gripped the obsidian railing, breath catching as he recognized the source.

"Eira," he whispered, disbelief threading his voice. "What have you done?"

Joy

Lysera gasped as the golden chamber around her flickered, the chalice in her hands slipping free and shattering against the marble floor. Nectar spilled and evaporated in a hiss of steam, the air thick with the scent of excess burned away.

She pressed a hand to her heart, pulse racing.

"She's burning," she murmured, awe and fear tangled together. "She's burning what she was."

Sorrow

Sorrow felt it as loss. Melora collapsed among her twilight gardens, the violets beneath her palms wilting instantly before curling inward, their petals darkening to ash. Tears welled without invitation, grief rising too fast and too sharp to be contained.

"No," she whispered. "This will break you, Eira. This is not how your story was written."

Revenge

Revenge felt it as promise. Vireth's blade slipped from his grasp and clattered against black marble. He turned toward the sky, lips parting in a slow, feral smile as understanding dawned.

"So she rises," he said softly, a slow smile creeping across his lips. "She rises against them."

Death

Across the spectrum of dominion, the Sovereigns

felt the same needle of disruption driven into their cores; Eira's transformation sent shockwaves through the bond that had always held them in equilibrium. But none of them understood the implications as clearly as Death.

Thaloré straightened, eyes burning with a darkened gold that had not been there before.

"She has touched something older than us," he said. "And if she moves again, Balance will not survive it."

Adrian

In the Temple of The Three, Adrian felt Eira before he understood what was happening. Her essence slammed into him without warning, heat and force and presence all at once, so overwhelming it drove the breath from his lungs. He doubled forward with a strangled sound, golden light erupting beneath his skin as the threads binding him flared in violent response.

Pain followed, sharp and bright, but beneath it—strength. The bindings shuddered, their hold loosening by degrees so small they would have gone unnoticed before. He laughed breathlessly, the sound torn from him by equal parts terror and relief.

"You did it," he whispered, voice raw. "You're coming."

For the first time since his capture, The Loom did not feel immutable. For the first time, it felt afraid.

Eira

Back in her realm, Eira felt everything. The Loom's recoil. The Fates' sudden, sharpened focus. Her siblings' shock echoing faintly across the bond they shared. And beneath it all, Adrian—warm and desperate and reaching for her with an intensity that cut through the chaos like light through smoke.

She did not flinch as the storm coiled around her, black and gold and crimson; the ground beneath her feet trembling as her realm struggled to adapt to what she had become. Her gown rippled like living shadow, the crown at her brow pulsing to the beat of her heart. The hunger inside her did not lessen. It sharpened.

She lifted her gaze to the vibrant sky, golden eyes reflecting the storm she had unleashed.

"Let them feel me," she said. And the world answered.

Gone was the Sovereign of Peace. In her place stood the Sovereign of Chaos.

CHAPTER 14
EIRA

The storm in Eira's realm had barely begun to settle when another presence pressed against it—cold, patient, and inevitable.

Death.

The sky split along a fault that had not existed moments before, not tearing so much as parting, as though the realm itself had recognized what approached and yielded in reluctant acknowledgment. Thaloré stepped through the opening without haste, his long black mantle trailing behind him like the shadows that obeyed him.

The constellations stitched into its fabric dimmed as he crossed the threshold, stars guttering out one by one beneath its folds. The air shuddered when his boots touched the altered ground. He inhaled once, slow and deliberate, and the storm hesitated—wind faltering, lightning thinning into distant veins of gold.

Death did not command Chaos. He did not need to. His mere presence was gravity enough.

"Chaos," Thaloré murmured, his voice low and measured, tasting the word with distaste as his expression tightened. "So this is what you have chosen."

Eira did not turn to acknowledge her oldest sibling. She stood at the heart of her transformed realm where the lake had once been glass-smooth and pale. Now its surface churned in slow spirals of black and gold, water catching fire only to extinguish itself again. The willows that once wept silver leaves now bore sharp black foliage that crackled faintly with energy, their roots lifting from the soil like claws testing their strength.

Her gown brushed around her legs, the crown atop her head pulsing faintly as it acknowledged its master. She stared up at the sky, gold eyes unblinking, her head tilting as she smiled. It was not a smile of happiness, but of cold satisfaction.

"You came quickly," she said quietly.

"When a realm screams," Thaloré replied, stepping closer, "I arrive."

"I did not call for you, Death." She spoke to him with a coldness Peace had never possessed.

"Perhaps not with words," he said gently. "But everything else you are ... called to me."

Her shoulders tightened. For a moment—only a moment—anguish crossed her face before she locked it away again. She would not show remorse for what she had become.

Thaloré crossed the obsidian field between them, boots crunching over petals that had once been pale and soft. The land recoiled around him, not in fear, but in recognition of the dominion he carried. Death did not threaten life here. He *ended* it when it was time. But not here ... never here.

"Look at me, Eira," he said quietly, his voice carrying the pull of a brother calling his sister back.

When she turned, he stopped short. Her hair burned red as fresh flame, threaded through with sparks of gold. Her eyes were no longer the calm blend of green flecked with gold he had known; but solid gold, molten and unwavering. He could feel her new form as her presence pressed outward, reshaping the air with every breath she took.

He knew that she was no longer Peace. Not anymore.

Something flickered across Thaloré's expression—grief, perhaps, or pride. Or both.

"Little sister," he whispered, "what have you done?"

"What I had to." Her voice cracked despite herself. "What they forced me to."

"The Fates are not kind to defiance, you know this!" His voice rose with an anger foreign to the quiet, calculated presence of Death.

"I am not asking them for kindness." Her voice sharpened. "I asked for Adrian."

Thaloré's eyes darkened. "And they refused. You knew that would be the way, Eira."

"They treated him like a threat. Like a disease to be contained." Gold flashed as tears welled in her eyes but refused to fall. "He is mine, Thaloré. He does not BELONG to them."

"No one is yours," he said softly. "Not even those you love."

She shook her head. "Do not speak to me of what is not mine." The storm stirred again, answering the fury beneath her words.

"So this is why Balance fractures," Thaloré said, gesturing to the writhing sky, the altered land. "Your power is reshaping you."

"It is not reshaping me," she said, stepping closer as flames ignited along her body, never burning her. "I am reshaping everything. I will break *everything*."

He braced, as if struck. "You were not meant to hold chaos," he said quietly. "It devours. It unravels—"

"It was mine long before Peace was forced upon me," she interrupted, defiantly.

Silence stretched between them, thick and unforgiving.

"You knew," she whispered, eyes widening; the realization cut deeper than any wound.

"I suspected," he admitted. "But I hoped ... I hoped I was wrong. Sometimes our natures contain a counterpart. But you were never meant to be—" he looked her over, sadness shadowing his expression as he gestured toward her, "*this.*"

"You hoped I would stay small," she said, a bitter laugh escaping her. "Contained and predictable. Peace, the Sovereign least likely to rebel."

"No." His voice softened. "I hoped you would never have to choose between your nature and your heart."

"Too late for that, brother," she snapped, her voice edged with steel.

Before he could answer, the realm shifted again.

Life arrived first. Zivael stepped through a curtain of green light, her presence blooming outward like a tulip bud forced through frozen ground. Grass tried to reclaim itself at her feet, curling up through cracked obsidian before withering under the strength of Eira's power. Zivael's expression held awe and grief in equal measure.

"Eira," she gasped. "What have you done to yourself?"

Sorrow followed. Melora emerged from a fold of shadow near the ruined garden. She fell to her knees almost immediately, fingers sinking into soil that pulsed with unfamiliar energy.

"This path ends in loss," Melora whispered, tears streaking freely. "It always does. Have you not learned from me, sister? From us both?" Her gaze flicked to Thaloré, and they shared a knowing look.

Then Fury arrived. Thamys tore through the sky like a blade through cloth, laughter ringing sharp and bright as he took in the altered realm. His eyes burned as he looked at Eira, admiration blazing openly across his face.

"There you are," he said, grinning. "I wondered how long it would take. Eira, you look absolutely flammable."

Revenge followed close behind. Vireth stepped from the shadow of a broken willow, gaze locked on Eira with something like reverence. "She did what none of us dared," he said quietly. "She chose."

Mercy arrived last. Elestra's presence settled like a balm that could not quite soothe the wound it touched. Pain accompanied her. Akria's silent and watchful eyes narrowed as she studied the fractures rippling through reality.

The only Sovereigns missing were Sedara, Caelus and Lysera; their absence did not go unnoticed. Eira knew Caelus would not come, for he had known which path she chose long ago. Such was the burden of Knowledge.

Thaloré turned slowly, taking in his siblings gathered in the storm. "This ends with war," he said, his voice carrying across the realm. "We all know it."

"I think it ends with truth," Vireth replied, "and hopefully bloodshed."

Thamys laughed again, his voice booming. "Then let it burn. Let them all burn!"

Eira turned away from them all, her voice cold and unyielding. "I will face you when the time comes. For now, I would like you to leave my realm."

Thaloré closed his eyes, exhaling deeply. "This is not the Peace I know."

"No," she said, a hard edge in her voice. "And I am not pretending to be that anymore. That which you knew is gone. Now *go*." She raised her hand and flames answered, surging into a solid wall of fire.

Her siblings each took one final look at their sister —no longer the Sovereign of Peace. Some smiled. Others made no effort to hide their disapproval. When they vanished, the storm rushed back in full force.

FAR AWAY, in the Temple of The Three, Adrian gasped as something tore through his bindings. Her essence hit him like lightning, gold and fire and something feral beneath it. Pain flared, sharp and blinding, but beneath it was undeniable power.

Threads snapped and he collapsed forward as one chain of light dissolved at his feet.

Adrian rose, smiling as he strained against the force holding him. With one final tug from a realm far away, The Loom began to lose its grip.

CHAPTER 15
ADRIAN

Adrian felt her before he heard her name echo through the threads. The sensation struck like a burst of heat, sharp at first, almost scorching; it spread outward in a slow tidal wave that stole the air from his lungs. He staggered, gripping the nearest pillar to keep himself upright as it rolled through him again, stronger this time, leaving his hands shaking.

"Eira ... " he whispered her name like a prayer finally answered.

Her essence poured into him, thick and molten, burning through every place The Fates had tried so desperately to contain. He bowed his head, squeezing his eyes shut as her presence surged through him in violent pulses, desperate and trembling with a hunger he had never felt from her before. This was not Peace, not a trace of the calm nature that used to invade his senses. It was something wild and ancient—something that answered him.

His chest rose and fell too fast, breath trembling as every thread woven through his body shuddered in response. He clutched at his sternum as if he could quiet the ache tunneling through him, as if holding himself together might keep him from breaking apart entirely.

Gods, he had never felt her so clearly. It wasn't just the power threading through him—though that alone made his bones hum—it was *her*. Her fear. Her fury. Her grief. Her desire. Her longing pressed against him like lips at his throat, beguiling and beautiful all at once. He pressed his forehead to the cold stone he clung to and whispered her name again, reverent and undone.

"Eira, you can do this, love. You *are* power, my love."

Then her transformation hit him—sudden and violent, like watching a star collapse and be reborn. Her power surged through his veins until he gasped, head thrown back, breath torn from him in a sound too close to a sob. Adrian felt it all: the heat of her hair as it burned red, the flash of gold as her eyes changed, the shadow of her gown as it darkened, the weight of her crown settling as if it formed above his own head.

His knees buckled. He caught himself against the

floor, fingers curling into nothing. "Don't," he pleaded hoarsely. "Don't do this without me."

The threads The Fates had woven through him strained, creaking under pressure they were never meant to withstand. Her power dragged at him, calling him, reaching for him with hands he could not see but felt everywhere. It was unbearable. It was exquisite. It was everything he always knew she could be. He had loved her quietly, wholly, and without expectation—a love too mortal for the power between them. But this was different. Now her essence sought him with a force that could reshape realms.

He doubled over as another wave tore through him, pain and beauty tangled together until he could no longer tell where one ended and the other began.

"I feel you," he whispered into the stone beneath him. "I feel all of you."

And he did. He felt the storm she created. The tremor of her breaking the threads. The scream she cast throughout realms. The moment she stopped being Peace. Her anger burned in his lungs, her sorrow bruised his throat, her longing dragged at him until he could taste her on the back of his tongue, warm and dangerous.

"Eira," he breathed, voice breaking completely. "Gods, I—"

He had never needed anything the way he needed

her in that moment. Not breath. Not freedom. Not even vengeance on the ones who had imprisoned him. He needed *her*, and he needed her *now*.

The threads around his wrists snapped—one, then another—golden light erupting from him as his power surged up his spine and burst behind his teeth, begging for release.

"You did it, Eira," he murmured, a savage grin taking shape. "We will bring them to their knees."

Another pulse surged through him—something that felt like a summons. Something within him answered, reaching for the pull that had always existed between them.

He stumbled forward, slamming his palms against the glowing barrier of his prison, longing alone nearly enough to break it. Her presence swelled again, flooding him so completely that he cried out, pressing his forehead to the wall.

"I can't stay here," he whispered, a wild laugh breaking from him. "I can't breathe without you."

Then the last binding dissolved. A blinding light exploded behind him, and Adrian stood unbound for the first time—trembling, transformed, and pulled toward her with a hunger that defied the will of gods.

"EIRA!" he shouted, voice rising, "Don't stop. Whatever you're doing— don't stop calling me."

Her essence hummed under his skin, answering

him. He closed his eyes and let himself feel her — just feel the sheer power and beauty of her — for one breath, two, three ...

And then he walked forward, toward the storm she had become.

CHAPTER 16
EIRA & ADRIAN

Eira stood at the center of what had once been her sanctuary, the storm coiling around her as though it recognized her as its axis. Power sparked at her fingertips in restless pulses, each surge sending a tremor through the ground beneath her feet. Her heart felt exposed, as if something vital had been torn free and left burning in its absence. Her pulse raced, uneven and wild, no longer answering to calm or restraint.

She could feel him. Not as a distant presence, nor an echo carried faintly through The Loom. The sensation was immediate and intimate, as if his heartbeat had become a part of her; beating in time with hers.

"Adrian," she commanded, "COME TO ME."

The name did not fade into the air, but transformed into a force that reached outward in search of its owner. Wind surged outward, whipping the lake into towering spirals. Water lifted and fell in great arcs, striking sparks from the threads that laced the sky. The land itself shuddered, every element reacting as though the sound of his name had struck a nerve.

Eira closed her eyes and turned inward, past the chaos she commanded now, past the remnants of Peace that still lingered like a memory. She reached for the bond between them. It was not a thread, not something woven by The Loom or granted by Balance. It was older than that. It was the love of a Sovereign.

The connection burned bright and gold the moment she touched it. Eira seized it without hesitation. The sky split above her with a sound like tearing metal—not her cry, but The Fates'. Their blended voices ripped through the storm, no longer distant or measured, but sharp with fury and alarm.

"Eira, stop!"

"This outcome was not permitted."

"He is not yours."

Their outrage pressed against her, heavy and insistent, but it only fed the pressure already coiling inside her. The storm tightened, spiraling inward toward the center of her will. Her gown lashed violently around her legs, flames snapping and curling like vipers, while her hair crackled with heat, red and gold igniting the air around her.

"I don't care," she said, the words torn from her. "Give him back to me, or I will TAKE him."

The Fates answered at once, their voices overlapping.

"You do not understand his purpose."

"You will destroy what was built."

"There is no path forward from this."

Eira's eyes burned brighter as fury sharpened into something cold. She lifted her chin. "You should have thought of that," she said, her voice steady though laced with anger, "before you decided for me."

She pulled and the world ruptured. The sky did not open like a doorway or tear like cloth. It split like a wound, exposing a stark white expanse beyond—a space that resisted form, shimmering as though it could not decide what it was meant to be. It was not a prison, and it was not freedom; but a realm suspended between realms, held in judgment and waiting.

Eira's breath caught painfully in her throat. Adrian was not imprisoned. He was being *held*—measured and preserved, like a blade laid bare on an altar waiting for a verdict that had not yet been delivered. A sound tore from her, raw and unguarded, caught between rage and heartbreak.

"ADRIAN!"

Through the rupture, she saw him standing on a narrow strip of light barely solid enough to bear him. Golden fissures climbed his arms, glowing beneath his skin, his breath harsh and uneven as his body trembled under the strain of her pull. Slowly, as though the universe itself resisted him, he lifted his head.

He looked undone, the harshness of his condition etched into every line of him—still beautiful, still glorious in his divine form. The moment recognition crossed his face, the bindings around his wrists flared and shattered, dissolving into drifting light.

"Eira," he gasped, her name breaking apart in his mouth like something sacred.

She reached for him through the wound in the sky and he reached back. The Fates' voices tore through the sky, panic breaking their careful order.

"Chaos cannot claim him!"

Eira bared her teeth as power surged sharp and lightning-fast beneath her skin. "I am not claiming him," she said, smirking, "I am calling him home."

When their hands locked, the realm exploded as light detonated outward. The tear sealed with a violent snap, and Adrian was hurled forward, his body crashing into her realm with enough force to shatter stone. Eira stumbled back as he collided with her—solid, warm, and undeniably real—his arms coming around her by instinct as both of them gasped, the pull between them finally releasing.

For one suspended breath, the storm fell silent. There were no Fates. No Loom. No Balance. There was only him. Only her.

CHAPTER 17
EIRA & ADRIAN

They stood in the heart of Eira's realm, staring at one another as though eons had passed since they had last seen each other. Adrian cupped her face with trembling hands, reverent and unsteady.

"You called me," he whispered, gazing into her eyes. "I could never deny you, Eira. You brought me back."

Her fingers clung to his shoulders, a sob tearing loose before she could stop it. "I did not know if—"

"I felt everything," he said, pressing his forehead to hers. "Every change, every fracture. Every breath you took while you transformed. I felt you. I can *feel* you now."

Her crown glimmered faintly as she settled into his embrace, his golden light reflected in her blazing eyes.

"Why were they holding you?" she asked, her voice tight with anger.

He swallowed hard, pressing his cheek to hers before answering. "I wasn't a prisoner, Eira," he spoke softly in her ear. "I was waiting."

"Waiting? Waiting for what?" Eira said, pulling back to look at him, anger flashing across her face.

"For The Architect to decide whether to kill me or use me," he answered, a muscle ticking in his jaw.

The words froze her blood. "Use you how?"

His hands slid to the sides of her neck, thumbs brushing her jaw as though anchoring himself. "The Architect never erased the old gods' bloodline," Adrian said quietly. "He hid it. Buried it in the mortal world and now he wants it back."

Eira nodded. The Watcher had already shown her the truth.

"The Architect wanted to see if my bloodline had fully awakened," he continued, "if I could become a vessel for the old gods trying to claw their way back."

Eira's throat tightened, as if his words had lodged there. "But you are not," she said anger slipping out before she could temper it. "You are not one of them."

"No," He said, as he reached for her hand, grip warm and unsteady. "But I am a crack they can use. The Fates told me that containment held only while nothing disturbed it. I guess *we* are the disturbance."

Adrian lifted her hand and pressed his lips to her

knuckles, adoration burning hot beneath his skin. "I never meant to be a danger to you," he said softly, closing his eyes for the briefest moment. "I can feel them, Eira; The Others in The Chasm. I feel their attention and their hunger. They know about you now."

Something in her went rigid. Her crown burned black, heat flaring at her temples as flames stirred within her veins.

"They cannot have you," she said, the words edged with something feral.

Adrian closed the last inch between them, resting his forehead against hers, his breath uneven. "If The Architect reaches me first, he'll use me—use what remains of them—to finish what he started. And if the old gods reach me first ... "

He exhaled, the sound breaking apart. They both knew what that could mean.

Eira's fingers curled into his shirt, gripping him as if the thought alone might pull him from her arms. "I won't let either of them touch you," she said, fierce and absolute.

His smile was brief, aching, and full of longing. "I know."

His voice deepened as he spoke again, roughened by something tender and desperate. "I felt you become Chaos. And gods, Eira ... " He shuddered, forehead still pressed to hers. "I've never felt anything so beautiful."

Her hand slid to the back of his neck, fingers

threading there as the connection between them hummed—heat and want tangled so tightly she could no longer separate them.

"Now that I've reached you first ... " she said, her meaning clear as the words trailed off.

Hope flickered across his face as he smiled. "Then maybe," he said, "we get to decide what happens next."

The realm shuddered beneath them; somewhere beyond sight, The Fates reacted. Balance strained and The Loom screamed in protest.

Eira pulled him closer, her voice trembling with defiance. "I will burn every realm before we are separated again."

Adrian laughed softly. "You already proved that. You are a remarkable goddess."

When their foreheads touched again, the connection between them did not merely burn. It roared.

Eira did not release him. Not immediately. For a moment, she simply stood there with her forehead pressed to his, the storm around them slowly finding a new rhythm, as if unsure whether it was meant to rage or kneel. Her hands remained fisted in the fabric at his back, anchoring herself to the proof of him—warm and real. She drew in a slow breath, steadying herself, and when she finally pulled back, her gaze did not soften.

"Come," she said.

It was not a command meant to be obeyed blindly. It was an invitation. The realm responded before Adrian could. The ground beneath their feet shifted, obsidian stone unfurling outward in smooth, deliberate lines. What had once been open sky drew inward, arches of dark crystal rising as though summoned by her will alone. Light bled through the structure—not gentle, not welcoming, but alive, pulsing in time with her heartbeat.

Adrian's eyes widened as he took it in. This was not the sanctuary she had lost, but something born of ruin and reclamation. Her palace rose around them like a crown settling into place; its walls formed of shadow and flame fused together, its ceilings impossibly high, the air humming with restrained power. Every surface seemed aware of her —of *them*—responding subtly as she moved, as though the structure itself leaned toward her presence.

She led him forward, her hand never leaving his. The contact burned—not painfully, but insistently—each step drawing the connection between them tighter. He could feel her still vibrating beneath the skin, chaos barely contained, and it made something within him ache with both reverence and want.

"You built this," he said quietly, awe slipping through the words.

"I did not build it," she replied without looking back. "I *claimed* it."

That earned a breathless sound from him that was almost a laugh. They passed through a vast chamber where the storm pressed against the outer walls, lightning tracing the edges of towering windows like veins of living fire. At the center stood a raised platform of dark stone, smooth and unmarked, waiting. The space felt private in a way that had nothing to do with walls—sealed not by isolation, but by intent.

Eira stopped there, then turned to face him. Up close, he could see the strain she carried—the way her power sat just beneath the surface of her skin. He noticed how her crown gleamed faintly as though still settling. Her eyes searched his face, sharp and unyielding, but beneath it all he felt the tremor she refused to show.

"You are here," she said, as if testing the truth of it aloud.

"I am," he answered, just as quietly.

Her hand lifted and came to rest against his chest. She did not push. She simply pressed her palm there, feeling the steady, frantic beat beneath it as her body shuddered in response.

"I felt you slipping away," she said. "And I do not ... I will not lose what is mine."

Something fierce and reverent crossed his face. His hand came up, cupping her wrist, grounding her touch without stopping it. "I wasn't slipping," he said. "I was waiting for you."

That was the point where restraint failed them both—where what had been coiled and contained finally broke free. The space between them collapsed into closeness so sudden it stole the air from both of them. Eira's power flared instinctively in response.

She lifted one hand, fingers curling through the air, and the obsidian altar behind them shuddered and reshaped itself. Stone flowed like liquid, darkening and widening until it formed a vast circular bed, its frame carved from blackened crystal. Above it, a floating canopy unfurled, threaded with a faint golden shimmer, as though starlight had been caught and stretched thin. The light spilled downward in soft embers, enclosing the space in a gentle glow.

One minute they stood in open space; the next, Eira gently but forcefully pushed him back onto the bed. Adrian barely had time to register the shift before Eira followed. The mattress dipped beneath their weight as she climbed onto the bed, bracing herself over him. Slowly, she slid the black gown over her body, tossing it to the floor. He swallowed, muscles tight beneath her, every instinct urging him forward while he waited—*for her*, always for her. She nodded, and that was all the confirmation he needed.

Adrian grabbed a fistful of her hair, pulling her close as he kissed her with a passion that threatened to consume them both. They were a whirlwind of limbs as Adrian stripped down to his bare form, sending his essence to tangle with hers. Eira gasped as she took in the sight of him, bare before her. Her eyes swept over every part of him, and a carnal desire filled the space where heartache once lived.

Their connection was powerful, something neither of them could contain. In the space they shared, nothing mattered but this moment; not her realm, nor any other. The only thing either of them were concerned with was connecting their souls and bodies.

Adrian's hands caressed her waist, fingers trailing a path to her neck before cupping her face as she stared at him intently with need so powerful he felt it in his bones.

"I do not need gentle, Adrian," Eira whispered breathlessly, biting her lip. "I need you."

His eyes darkened as he caressed her cheek once more, sliding his hands gently to her throat. His grip tightened just a little, feeling what she needed from him before he claimed her mouth. He lifted her off him, flipping her onto her back before settling over her. His eyes caressed her skin as they took in the perfection of her form. Her body flushed as his gaze raked over her face, her breasts and lower. His hands roamed her body, exploring her sensual curves as he traced his fingertips up her torso.

She moaned his name, her neck arching in pleasure as he placed kisses along her jawline, trailing down her neck, then to her breasts.

Adrian hummed, his mouth never leaving her body. He groaned as his body eagerly anticipated claiming her. Awareness sparked along his nerves, every one of them drawn tight and waiting. Golden light spilled from his skin, challenging her. Eira erupted in answer, bright flames surging around them without heat or harm.

"Make love to me, Adrian," she purred huskily.

The air around them stilled as they connected, pressure building until it burst with desire. Eira moaned his name like a quiet prayer as Adrian pressed heated kisses against her mouth, eyes never leaving hers as he made love to her with an intensity that could no longer be controlled. Ripples of power spread throughout the room—throughout the realm—as they moved in sync, both consumed by primal need.

"I love you," Eira whispered before he captured her mouth in a deep kiss—consuming her, the flames, *everything*. Power rolled off them both in quiet waves, heat and flame woven together, pressing in until there was room for nothing else.

"You changed everything," he murmured, his body

pressed so close to hers it felt as if they were one entity.

"So did you," she whispered, running her fingers through his hair as she took everything he gave, body vibrating with love, power, and ecstasy.

For a long moment, they stayed like that—no rush, no breaking point—just the quiet intensity of two forces finally standing on the same side of the world. Outside, the storm continued to coil and churn, but within the palace, within the space she had claimed for herself and now for him, everything held.

CHAPTER 18
EIRA

Eira had known the world was unraveling long before she ever touched Adrian's thread. She had felt the fracture in Balance—subtle, persistent, easy to dismiss if one was not born of it. The signs were there for those willing to notice, but her siblings brushed aside her unease. The Fates offered no warning. The Architect remained silent, distant as a sealed horizon, watching without intervention.

But she had felt it.

She had felt it in the pauses between seconds, in the stillness that was never truly still, in the way the threads shivered whenever Adrian's presence brushed against their edges. Balance had strained long before it cracked. Now, there was no mistaking it, because the unraveling was no longer subtle. It was a roar.

Her realm lurched beneath her feet as another fracture split the sky. The air vibrated with a sharp, keening hum that set her teeth on edge, the sound of something vast being pulled too far, too fast. Balance was not merely strained—it was choking.

Adrian stepped closer, his presence immediate and grounding as his hand brushed the back of her arm. Chaos roared through her veins, eager to be unleashed, and his touch anchored it—proof that even now, she chose when the world would break.

"It is worse," she said, resisting the tug from Chaos. The time to unleash it would come—but not now.

"You always knew it would be," Adrian replied, his voice low but steady.

Eira did not deny it. There was no need. The lake at the heart of her realm—once a mirror of stillness—reflected truth without suppression. When she lifted her hand, the water rose to meet her touch, its surface shifting in quiet recognition. Her power was volatile, yes—but it was no longer at odds with the world she commanded. The realm she had reshaped recognized its Sovereign.

"It is accelerating," she said, her voice calm despite the storm coiling beneath it. "I held this together once. Even when no one believed me. Even when The Fates insisted Balance was intact."

Her gaze sharpened. "Now I see what they refused to let me feel. What has always been hidden."

Adrian turned fully toward her. "What do you see?"

Eira did not hesitate. "I see the beginning of collapse."

The words had barely settled when the air behind her parted. Shadow rippled across the sky, folding inward as Thaloré stepped through the veil. Death's robes trailed darkness that drank the light around it, his expression tight, drawn with something she rarely saw in him. Fear.

"Eira," he said quietly, "your realm is destabilizing the realms beyond it."

Before Eira could answer, heat and perfume flooded the air as Sedara emerged, her presence unmistakable. Pleasure's silk robes snapped like banners caught in a storm, her usual confidence replaced with keen alertness.

"I suppose I will have to agree with our brother yet again," Sedara said, her gaze sweeping the horizon. The familiar purr in her voice was gone, morphed into something precise. "The mortal realm is reacting. Storms are forming where they shouldn't, and fear is bleeding through everything."

Others followed in rapid succession. One by one, the Sovereigns gathered, forming a wide circle within

Eira's realm, their attention fixed on her as though she were the axis upon which the world now turned.

Adrian shifted beside Eira. She felt it immediately—the way the realm subtly adjusted to accommodate him, the way the threads overhead shuddered and resettled around his presence. Several of the Sovereigns noticed it and their attention turned.

"Ah," Thamys said quietly, his gaze sliding to Adrian, "the demigod."

Eira moved without hesitation, stepping half a pace in front of Adrian. Not defensively, but deliberately. The message was unmistakably clear.

"He was never the cause of this," she said. "And he remains with me."

No one challenged her.

Thaloré inclined his head slightly. "We are not here to claim him, Eira."

"I know," she said. Her smile was thin as a blade, her golden eyes burning steadily. "If you were, you would not have crossed into my realm uninvited."

All of the Sovereigns understood the implied threat. Sedara's lips curved faintly in approval.

Thaloré nodded before speaking again. "Something has awakened," he said, tension threading through his voice.

Eira lifted her chin. Her crown gleamed faintly against her red hair, responding to the other Sovereigns.

"I am aware," she said evenly. "The Architect has been interfering for some time."

The Sovereigns shifted at that. Whether they recognized the Titans' embers or their tie to Adrian, Eira did not test it. Some truths were more dangerous once spoken aloud.

Thaloré studied her closely, his gaze sharp and assessing. "You speak with certainty."

"I speak with experience," Eira replied.

She looked at their faces, and could feel the Sovereigns had not come to judge her. They came because the mortal realm was no longer behaving as it should. Something had changed.

"The Architect will wake," Thaloré said, his voice measured, but strained. "The signs are unmistakable."

Eira did not look away. "He already is," she replied.

That drew their attention immediately. Sedara's gaze narrowed, interest cutting through her unease. Mercy stilled. Melora's sorrow deepened into something heavier, more grim.

"Then you understand what is at stake," Elestra said carefully.

Something unreadable crossed Eira's face. "I understand what has *always* been at stake," she said. "What none of us wanted to name."

A ripple of tension moved through the circle, but she continued.

"The fracture did not begin with my love for Adrian," Eira said slowly, "nor my transformation."

Her gaze swept them, one by one. "It began long before any of us transgressed against The Loom. Long before Balance faltered. Before we decided silence was safer than scrutiny."

The air tightened at those words. Even the wind stilled, as though listening as the Sovereigns murmured their agreement. The sky above them fractured again, a thin vein of gold splitting across the clouds before sealing itself shut. Adrian's fingers brushed hers, letting her know he was present and unafraid.

Thaloré spoke the truth none of them wished to avoid. "The Architect is awake."

"Then let him come," Eira said sharply. Flame unfurled around her and Adrian at her command. It rose as a living barrier, precise and deliberate, shaped by her will alone. The realm responded immediately to her. Power surged outward in a controlled wave, not destructive, but ready—Chaos held in deliberate check, waiting to be unleashed.

Adrian stepped fully beside her, golden fissures along his skin brightening in answer. "We are not unprepared."

None of the Sovereigns argued, but their silence said everything. They knew a war was coming.

"If you want the truth," Eira said, meeting each Sovereign's eyes without yielding, "go to the ruins. Learn the truth you have all avoided."

CHAPTER 19
EIRA

Eira sat upon her throne, a towering seat of carved black onyx whose edges were sharp and whose surface hummed faintly beneath her palms. She took in the palace around her, still adjusting to its presence—so unlike the realm she had once shaped as Peace. That place had been soft and delicate. This new realm was none of those things.

Golden pillars rose toward a fractured sky, their surfaces etched with spiraling veins that shimmered like starlight caught in molten metal. Marble walls caught glints of her power as they shifted faintly, alive in a way stone had never been before. Broad staircases unfurled in sweeping curves, their balustrades carved with symbols shaped by intention.

The floors were black marble, streaked through with veins of red-gold fire that moved beneath the surface like a living current. Flames curled around the base of the throne in controlled ribbons, rising along the steps without scorching them. Her gown spilled in dark waves down the sides of the throne, merging seamlessly with the shadows at her feet as if they had always belonged to her.

Adrian stood beside her, one hand resting against the arm of the throne, the other loose at his side. Golden fissures traced his skin like constellations, pulsing faintly in rhythm with the fire that circled her seat of power. He had never looked more divine, and the sight of it sent tremors through her heart. His gaze kept returning to her, as though anchoring himself to her presence alone could hold at bay whatever strained beyond the boundaries of her realm.

Eira brushed her fingers against his, and he looked down at her touch. The fierce pull between them tightened instantly—familiar and insatiable.

"I cannot believe you are here with me," she murmured, the words edged with a love so fierce it startled her as she looked up at him.

Adrian's fingers wrapped around hers, firm and certain. "Neither can I," he said. "But I am here." He leaned closer, his voice low and unwavering. "I will stand with you until there is nothing left that can pull us apart."

Something stirred at that; within her a slow, ancient resonance answered his words. She was *his*, and he was *hers*. She smiled at him, content with the certainty that she would reduce every realm to ash before she let anyone separate them again.

Adrian stepped closer, brushing a stray strand of red hair back from her face with a gentleness that undid her. She lifted her hand, tracing the glowing fissures along his arm.

"You are warm," she whispered.

"So are you," he smiled, leaning down to place a soft kiss on her lips.

She opened her mouth to speak when the flames around the throne flickered violently. The tension between them thickened in an instant as they paused at the intrusion within her realm.

A cold pressure slid through the air, sharp and sudden, like a blade drawn quickly from its sheath. Adrian stiffened and Eira straightened at once, her hand snapping away from his arm as instinct coiled tight within her. Fire and lightning gathered in her hand, twisting together into a living core of power, not unleashed but held in readiness, a warning to anything that dared cross into her realm.

The palace fell silent—not the quiet of calm, but the suffocating stillness of a predator entering the room. Every flame lifted in defense, while shadows drew inward, coiling and sharpening as if preparing to strike. The air thickened against her skin, heavy and unyielding, the weight of something ancient announcing itself without a single word. Then a presence settled into her mind—old, patient, and vast. It did not announce itself, did not press or intrude. It simply *was*, filling the space with an authority that had shaped worlds long before she existed. Eira knew instantly who it was.

The Architect had come.

"So," he said—not aloud, but everywhere at once. *"This is the answer you chose."*

Eira's fingers tightened against the arms of her throne. Adrian's hand came to her shoulder, instinctive and protective, the gold along his skin flaring brighter.

The presence shifted, considering her. *"Chaos reborn,"* he continued, his attention rolling over her with chilling precision, *"wearing Peace's skin."*

The flames surged upward in a column of black-gold light before snapping back into rigid stillness. Adrian stepped fully in front of Eira, placing himself between her and the presence of The Architect pressing into the room. Instinct drove him forward, divine blood flaring as it met an immovable force. He did not retreat. The gold along his skin flared violently in warning, embers stirring beneath the surface as his blood answered in defiance.

"You don't touch her," he said, his voice tight, "You don't get to stand here and weigh her worth."

The Architect regarded Adrian next, cool and exacting.

"Ah, Adrian Lysander," he observed. *"As predictable as your bloodline."*

Eira rose to her feet in a single fluid motion, fire unfurling around her ankles in deliberate ribbons. "Show yourself," she demanded, her voice steady with restrained fury.

A low, measured sound rippled through the palace, something between amusement and acknowledgment.

"Not yet," The Architect replied. *"Observation precedes intervention."*

Her pulse thundered. "Why?" she demanded. "Why wait? Why allow the world to fracture?"

The pressure intensified, heavy enough to make the marble beneath her feet creak.

"Because containment only reveals its limits under strain," The Architect answered calmly. *"And I wished to see what would happen when pressure was applied to every boundary at once."*

Adrian sucked in a sharp breath. Cracks raced faintly along the walls as Eira's power surged in response.

"And now?" she asked quietly. "Have you decided, father?"

A pause followed, ancient and deliberate. *"Yes,"* The Architect said at last. *"I have decided because you chose to act. I wish you would have chosen differently, but the time has passed for that."*

The palace groaned as though bracing itself. Beyond the walls, the threads that bound the realms shuddered violently, stretched to their limits.

"I will come for what was never meant to endure," The Architect continued, his attention locking onto them both. *"And I will finish what was interrupted."*

Then the pressure lifted. The flames collapsed back into motion as the walls exhaled. The palace trembled once, settling into itself as the presence withdrew beyond the veil of her realm.

Adrian turned to her slowly, his eyes narrowed, the gold along his skin blazing.

"So this is it," he said, his fingers curling once as power stirred beneath his skin. "He'll come for us."

Eira lifted her chin, the crown upon her head burning bright. "He will," she replied, her voice unwavering. "And I am done hiding from him."

The Architect's presence receded at last like a sealed wound. The throne room trembled in its absence, stone and flame settling uneasily as if the palace itself were bracing for what would follow. Eira stood before her throne, her crown flickering with black-gold firelight. Flames gathered at her feet, rising and falling in time with her pulse, no longer wild but alert.

Adrian did not speak. He watched her from where he stood beside the throne, noting the tension in her shoulders; his eyes caught the brief tremor in her hands before they steadied, the way she lifted her chin with quiet, furious resolve. The golden fissures along his skin brightened subtly as his attention sharpened, then he moved. One step forward, onto the lower step of the dais, placing himself directly before her throne. Close enough to feel the heat radiating from her. Close enough to see the faint quiver in her fingers.

Eira's gaze met his, molten gold and unflinching.

"Adrian," she said softly, her brow furrowing.

He met her gaze steadily, brushing a loose tendril of hair from his face as he lowered himself to his knees. He kneeled not because she demanded it or because she was Chaos, but because he chose to meet her power without fear. Because watching her stand against The Architect had broken something open inside him that had been held tight for far too long.

He bowed his head briefly, but when he spoke, his voice was steady, thick with conviction. "I choose you," he said quietly. "Not Balance. Not The Fates. Not The Architect. I choose you, Eira. My loyalty, my heart, my *everything*, is yours to command."

He lifted his gaze to meet hers. "From the moment

I saw you in that coffee shop, I knew. It was always going to be you."

Eira inhaled sharply as her essence surged in response. Flames around the throne rose in spiraling arcs, answering her pulse. She reached out, fingertips trembling, and brushed her hand along his cheek. He leaned into the touch instinctively, grounding himself in it.

"I do not want your worship," she said softly, "I only want you."

"I know," he replied. "You want honesty. You want choice." He lifted his hand and curled his fingers around hers, pressing her palm to his face. "And I am choosing you. Not because you are Chaos, but because you are Eira. Because you are *mine*."

Something inside her gave way in release. Golden light flared beneath her fingers, and the throne room shuddered as her heart beat once, then again. Eira lifted her other hand, and the space beside her throne rippled like disturbed water. Marble cracked as gold surged upward, twisting and shaping itself under her command. Light gathered into form, deliberate and precise. A second throne rose beside her own. Its edges were sharp and sure, its curves smooth and intentional. It echoed her throne without mimicking it. This was not an offering. It was a declaration of who and what Adrian was to her.

Adrian stared, unable to look away, his mouth parting slightly.

"I don't want you kneeling before me," Eira said, her voice breaking slightly. "I want you beside me, Adrian."

The golden throne settled into place with a resonant chime as Adrian rose slowly, her hand still in his. He looked at the throne, then at her, then back again.

"For me?" he asked, incredulity flickering across his face. She lifted his hand to her lips. "Yes for you ... for us."

He exhaled as though releasing a breath he had been holding for years, then lowered himself onto the throne. The moment he sat golden light flared around him, acknowledging him. Light rippled through his body as the throne accepted him.

He reached for her hand again, and she took it without hesitation. Their fingers intertwined and for a moment, nothing else mattered. Not The Architect. Not The Fates. Not the unraveling beyond the realm.

"You chose me," Eira said quietly as a tear slid down her cheek.

"I did," Adrian replied, his gaze unwavering. "I would choose you in every lifetime."

Silence stretched between them, heavy with things unspoken as Eira's gaze fixed on something beyond him. Adrian noticed immediately.

"What is it?" he asked. "What's turning in your mind?"

She looked down at their joined hands before lifting her gaze.

"I have a plan," she said.

Adrian's brows knit briefly. "Eira."

"I am tired," she continued. "Tired of being told what I am. What I must protect. I held the world together for millennia, and no one cared until you became a threat."

His jaw tightened. "So what's the plan?"

"I am done waiting for someone to decide our fate," she said. "I am done being a piece on anyone's board."

She leaned toward him, crown silhouetted in fire. "I am going to take back what he stole."

"What did he steal?" Adrian asked.

She lifted her hand, palm open. "Choice."

Understanding flickered across his face, followed by awe and fear entwined.

She rose from her throne and flames surged in recognition as she stood between the thrones.

"There are mortals whose blood still remembers the old gods," she said. "Not many, but just enough. Their influence seeped into the mortal realm when The Architect fractured them."

She met his gaze. "Their blood carries embers.

Fragments The Architect never truly destroyed. If I find them, I can wake what exists in The Chasm."

Adrian nodded slowly. "You want to wake them."

"I want to give them a voice again," she corrected. "And if they wish to rise ... they will rise through me if they wish to exist peacefully within The Loom's design."

He watched her carefully. "You don't have to do this alone."

"No," she replied, smiling. "I do not. My first stop will be the mortal realm. Do you not miss that place?"

"I miss the food," he said dryly, then sobered. "And yes. I'm coming with you."

"You will," she said softly.

He leaned forward, his voice low and unwavering as he whispered, "I'm yours."

Eira smiled and her eyes burned brighter as she answered, "I know."

They sat side by side—two forces shaped by different eras—as her realm echoed their shared heartbeat.

"So what now?" Adrian asked, looking up at her.

Eira did not look away. "Now we prepare for war."

Adrian's mouth curved slowly, nodding at her as he took in the sheer beauty of a goddess preparing for every possibility.

"You are ... magnificent. Come here," Adrian said

quietly, pulling her gently towards him as his eyes darkened with desire.

Eira moved to the front of his throne and slid languidly onto his lap, draping her legs over the side. She looked down at him, lids lowering as she drank in the sight of him. Adrian was here, and he would rule this realm with her. *Her demigod.* The thought caused a rush of power to surge within her.

His eyes studied her features, lingering as they did back when he would sketch her. His hand slid to her face, gently caressing her cheek and she leaned into the strength of his touch. Realms could collapse, everything could burn, and Eira would care only about this moment.

Adrian slid his free hand along her thigh causing tingles to rise along her spine as Eira brought her lips to his. The kiss started off slow, passion rising as they savored the tether that had always been there.

"You are mine," Adrian said huskily, breaking their connection. "Always."

"Always." Eira echoed, breathlessly.

Endless moments passed as their need overtook them–fire and light flaring– building to a steep and final crescendo.

CHAPTER 20
THE MORTAL REALM

The first sign arrived in the mortal realm as a dream. It did not announce itself with trumpets or prophecy, the way the end of the world was always imagined by mortals. It arrived the way most disasters did: quietly, in private, in the soft hours before dawn when no one was looking for it and almost everyone was defenseless.

A woman in a fourth-floor apartment sat upright in bed with a scream that scraped her throat raw. Her sheets tangled around her legs and her hair clung damply to her forehead. The room was dark except for the faint glow of a digital clock on the nightstand and the pale smear of streetlight leaking through the blinds.

Her heart hammered as if it had been running without her. She pressed a hand to her chest, expecting to find the steady rhythm she had known for years. Instead, it answered her touch with an uneven double beat that made her stomach drop. She held still, listening to her own body as if it had become unfamiliar terrain.

Something had been in her dream. Something enormous. She tried to grasp the details, but they became murky the moment she reached for them, leaving only the residue of sensation. Cold water. The taste of iron. The feeling of being watched by something. She remembered a name, but it was not a name she could repeat in waking without her tongue stumbling. It had sounded older than language, a sound shaped by the mouth of the earth itself.

A hand rose out of a dark sea. She could still see it if she closed her eyes; it was not a human hand, but something not of this world. It was too large, too graceful, its fingers long and slow, lifting from the water as if the water had been a veil it could part. Behind it, eyes opened beneath the earth; not eyes with lids and lashes, but a presence that became aware.

She shuddered hard enough that the bedframe creaked. Her husband stirred beside her, rolling over without opening his eyes. "You okay?" he mumbled, voice thick with sleep.

She stared at him, grateful for the sound of a human voice. "I had a nightmare," she whispered.

"What about?"

"I ... I do not know." That was what frightened her most. The terror remained, but the story did not. "It was just ... wrong."

He made a comforting sound and fell back into sleep as easily as if fear were something you could turn off with a sigh. She sat upright for a long time, still lost in thought. When she finally lay back down, she kept her eyes open and watched the ceiling. She did not drift again because she did not trust her own mind.

In the morning, she would wake feeling stretched and tilted, as if the world inside her had shifted one inch to the left and never corrected. She would drink coffee and stare at her phone and tell herself it was stress, that it was nothing, that dreams were only dreams.

She would not know it was a Titan's echo sliding through her sleep. She would not know she had spoken a name out loud in the dark. She would only know she felt wrong.

And she was not the only one.

Across the ocean, the second sign came with a song. A boy, no older than six, stood barefoot at the edge of his backyard with his pajama sleeves pushed up to his elbows. The grass was stiff with frost and a thin line of sunrise brightened the horizon; the sun itself was still hidden, and the air had the sharp bite of winter. He hummed as he stared at the sky.

His mother rinsed dishes in the kitchen sink, listening through the opened screen door, the way parents listen to their children when everything is fine —half-aware, reassured by familiar noise. The tune was soft at first, a gentle repetition that made her think of nursery rhymes and cartoons. It had a sweetness to it, almost pretty. Then it caught in her ear. Not because it was loud, but because it was wrong. It turned in on itself in a way that made her skin prickle. It carried a gravity no child should be able to invent. It felt like a memory, not a song, and the longer she listened, the more she realized she did not recognize a single note of it.

She turned off the faucet and wiped her hands on a dish towel as she walked to the door. "What are you humming, sweetheart?"

The boy did not turn. He swayed slightly, as if the sound were moving through him rather than coming from him. His gaze remained fixed on the brightening sky.

"Who taught you that?" she asked, softer now.

The boy finally looked back over his shoulder. His wide eyes were unfocused, as though he had not fully climbed out of sleep. His face was blank in the way that was unnatural.

"It comes from the dark," he said simply.

His mother went very still and for a moment, the air around the boy seemed to tighten. The frost on the grass glittered as if it had caught a strange light. Then the boy blinked and the humming stopped. His shoulders relaxed as if a string had been cut.

"What?" the mother whispered.

He frowned. "I'm hungry," he said, suddenly ordinary, back to himself.

She stared at him for a long beat, trying to hold onto the melody so she could repeat it later to prove to herself it had happened. She opened her mouth, then closed it again. The song was gone. Not forgotten the way you forget a tune you cannot quite place. Gone as if it had never existed, as if her mind had been made to release it.

She walked toward her son slowly, heart beating too hard. She tucked hair behind his ear with trembling fingers and forced herself to smile. "Come on," she said. "Let's get breakfast."

He ran into the house without looking back while she stood in the doorway for a moment longer, staring at the sky as if it might offer her an explanation. Her hands shook for the rest of the morning, and she could not have said why.

Across the country, in a university library, the third sign arrived in the most mundane way possible—exhaustion. Three scholars had fallen asleep at their desks at different tables, each with a stack of books open in front of them. Finals week, deadlines, grant applications; the usual reasons people slept in libraries. Their bodies had given up before their minds did.

They woke within the same minute. All three jerked upright with a gasp, hands flying to their throats as if they had been drowning. Their eyes were wide, pupils blown. Their breaths came fast and shallow. For a moment, each stared at the pages in front of them as if the text had become incomprehensible overnight. Then, slowly, they looked up.

Their gazes found one another across a sea of work tables. They were all complete strangers to one another. None of them had spoken, and yet the expression on each face was the same. A raw, startled recognition that made their stomachs drop.

One of them, a woman with her hair pulled into a messy bun and ink smudged across the side of her hand, reached for the pen beside her notebook. Her fingers moved before her mind caught up and she wrote a word.

Nerithios.

The letters were neat and deliberate. The moment she finished the final stroke, pain shot through her palm as if the pen had burned her. She dropped it with a startled yelp. The pen clattered across the desk and rolled onto the floor.

Her breath came out in a shaky laugh that sounded wrong. "What the hell," she whispered.

Her colleague at the next table glanced over, annoyed, then froze when he saw her face. "Are you okay?"

She shook her head. "I don't ... I don't know why I wrote that."

"What is it?" he asked as he got up and approached her table, peering down at the notebook.

She covered the page with her hand as if the word were dangerous. "I don't know," she said again, and the helplessness in her voice startled her.

Across the aisle, one of the other scholars stood abruptly, chair scraping loud against the floor. He grabbed his coat as if he might flee. His face had gone pale. He kept shaking his head like someone trying to clear water from his ears.

The third scholar, a graduate student with dark circles under her eyes, stared at her own hands as if expecting to find them changed. Her lips moved silently, repeating something she could not quite hear.

Outside the library window, leaves spiraled upward instead of falling. It only lasted a few seconds; a small, impossible reversal. Then gravity corrected itself and the leaves resumed their slow descent. No one inside saw it, but the air in the library felt wrong for the rest of the night.

THE FRACTURES WERE small at first. They did not arrive as a single catastrophe, instead as a pattern of tiny wrongnesses scattered across the world. The world held itself together, but barely. That was how it always began, when something old stirred. Not with destruction, but with remembering.

For mortals, memory was soft and unreliable. It faded and changed and bent to protect them from pain. For the things that lived under creation, memory was a force. It pressed against the present until the present was forced to make room.

The approaching presence was older than anything mortals could conceive in their minds. It did not move with haste. It moved with inevitability. When it shifted, the world noticed, even if no one could explain what they were noticing. It stirred now for two reasons. First, because Chaos had awakened. Second, because she was looking for them.

EIRA LIFTED HER HEAD ABRUPTLY. She had been standing in the dim quiet of Adrian's apartment, listening to the city's threads with her eyes closed, when something rolled through the weave like a distant wave. It was not the tug of a single mortal thread. This was broader—a global tremor that carried the weight of many minds brushing against the same memory at once.

Across the room, Adrian straightened as if he had been pulled by an unseen force.

"You felt that," Eira said quietly.

Adrian nodded once, jaw tight. "Like the air changed," he murmured. "Like something shifted everywhere—all at once."

Eira stepped toward the window and looked out at the city. Threads of light and shadow lay over the world like a web, some taut, some fraying, some glowing faintly as if heated from within. It was subtle, but it was there. Her entire being ached with the sheer scale of it.

It would have been easier if the signs were loud. Easier if the world cracked in half all at once and she could point to a single catastrophe and name it. Instead, the universe was doing what it always did when something ancient pressed upward.

It was whispering first.

Adrian came up behind her, close enough that she felt his warmth against her back as he pressed a gentle kiss to her neck.

Finally, he spoke. "How many?" he asked.

Eira did not answer immediately. She let her

senses stretch outward again, beyond the city, beyond the borders of the mortal world that mortals believed were fixed. She reached for the pulses she had begun to hear and found them like distant lanterns across a dark sea.

"Too many," she said wearily. "Enough to change the air."

Adrian exhaled slowly, the sound tight with awe and dread. "They are waking."

Eira's gaze remained on the sky as she nodded. "They are remembering."

He was silent for a moment. Then, softly, "And The Architect?"

She felt it then, like a cold fingertip tracing the back of her neck. He did not enter the room, not as a presence she could see or confront; still she felt the weight of The Loom shift, searching. Her barrier held. Their conversations remained sealed within it, hidden from the threads that governed all else. For now.

She allowed herself one measured breath and held to the certainty that followed. The Architect did not yet know what they were planning.

"He is watching," she said. "He will move when he thinks he must."

Adrian's voice lowered. "Do you think he already knows you found the first ember?"

Eira considered. The Architect's attention was calculated. He did not react to every tremor or he would be forever chasing ripples. But she also knew he could feel shifts in The Loom. He could feel when a thread tightened or when a pattern changed.

"If he does not know yet," she said slowly, "he will soon."

Adrian nodded once. "Then we do not waste time."

Adrian's arms slid around her waist, grounding her without hesitation. He rested his cheek against her shoulder, his breath steady and warm where it brushed her skin, and she felt her own breathing slowly fall into rhythm with his. Eira closed her eyes and covered his hand where it rested at her waist, her fingers tightening around his in quiet reassurance. She drew in a measured breath, knowing she would need every ounce of her strength for what came next.

SOMEWHERE DEEP BENEATH CREATION, in the darkness where The Chasm lapped at the edges of the world, something ancient shifted again, turning toward the sound of Chaos like a creature orienting to a familiar call.

Eira opened her eyes.

"We do not have much time," she said, and this time, when she spoke, it was not a warning.

It was a promise.

CHAPTER 21
EIRA

Eira felt the pressure before the barrier wavered. It was not pain or fear, but a steady insistence against her awareness, like fingers testing the edge of a sealed door. She stood near the window of Adrian's apartment, her gaze fixed on the city below as if anchoring herself to something familiar. The skyline glowed beneath a low haze, traffic threading through the streets in orderly lines. Mortals moved through their lives unaware that the rules governing their world were tightening.

"He is trying to penetrate my barrier," she said quietly. "I can feel it."

The tremor in her voice made Adrian's spine stiffen. He crossed the room without hesitation and positioned himself between her and the open window, his body angling instinctively as if that alone could shield her. The city lights cast his shadow over her, long and solid, grounding.

"We need to go," he said. "Back to your realm. Now."

She shook her head once. "*Our* realm. And no."

He turned fully toward her, eyes searching her face. "Eira."

"You need to stay here." She finally pulled her gaze from the horizon to meet his. "My siblings are close. I can feel them."

The golden fissures along his throat and cheekbones brightened in response, molten light stirring beneath his skin. "I'm not leaving you alone while he's watching."

She stepped closer until the space between them disappeared. The city noise blurred, The Architect's distant pressure sharpening at the edges of her senses. She pressed her forehead to his, fingers curling around his wrists.

"Please, Adrian," she said, placing a hand against his solid chest. "My siblings do not come to the mortal realm unless it matters. Let me speak to them. We will leave right after."

The words were softly spoken, but landed with quiet authority. Adrian closed his eyes and exhaled slowly. His jaw tightened, then released. The hand at her hip trembled once before steadying, his thumb tracing the fabric of her dress as if memorizing it.

"I hate this," he murmured. "I'm letting you know right now, I don't agree with this."

"I know," she said gently. "But we do not need more attention tonight. I will talk to them and come back. It will not take long."

He did not bother hiding his disapproval. He caught her by the waist and pulled her close, pressing a kiss to her forehead anyway. "Are you always this stubborn?" he asked, forcing lightness into his tone.

She heard what he did not say. The concern threaded beneath it.

"That is an argument we have been having since the beginning," she replied.

He huffed out a breath that was half laugh, half curse. His fingers slid to the back of her neck, grounding. "Come back quickly," he said. "No more separation."

"I will," she promised. "Just a moment."

Reluctance settled into his expression before he kissed her once more, gentle and deliberate, then stepped back. Light gathered along the veins of gold beneath his skin. The air folded, creasing reality itself, and she was gone.

"Eira."

A low, commanding voice spoke her name, one she would have recognized anywhere. She turned.

Thaloré stood at the edge of the street, half caught in shadow, twilight clinging to him like a second skin. His presence drew silence in its wake, and the world seemed to remember him as he moved closer. Cars still passed, people still walked, but their noise dulled into irrelevance, as though the city understood it was not meant to speak over Death.

"You could have waited," she said, steadying herself.

"I do not wait for Chaos," he replied. "Chaos comes when it chooses." He paused, listening beyond her hearing. "Walk."

Before she could answer, the world folded. Streetlights blinked out as concrete and glass blurred, edges dissolving as time shifted its rhythm. Gravity loosened its hold, and the mortal realm slipped away. Death's realm unfolded beneath her feet.

Eira followed Thaloré in silence, taking in the restrained beauty of his domain. "Why bring me here?" she asked. "I did not wish to leave Adrian."

"Because someone wished to see you," he said. "And because this is the one place where The Architect's gaze is weakest. Like you, I have my own barriers."

Light gathered ahead, threading itself into form as Caelus stepped into the clearing, twilight and starlight woven into his robes.

"Caelus," Eira said. "What are you up to?"

"We need to speak with you, sister," he replied gently. "And attempt to sway your judgment."

"I doubt anything can sway me at this point," Eira said coolly. "But speak. What do you need, brothers?"

Caelus did not waste time. "The Architect is not displeased because you transformed," he said. "He is displeased because you remember. Chaos remembers the gods he banished. And we know why he wants Adrian."

Eira smiled faintly. They knew, then. The lie of the old gods being truly unmade had finally cracked. She thought of the child she had sensed earlier, the golden warmth beneath mortal skin.

"You touched an ember today," Caelus continued. "When you have all of them, you will be able to open The Gate."

"The Gate," she repeated, her brow furrowing.

"The place before The Chasm," he said. "When the embers align, it will answer you."

"And the Titans will wake?"

"Enough to remember who tried to erase them," Caelus replied. "We can only hope time has tempered their rage."

"I only want to restore Balance the right way," Eira said. "I want Adrian safe."

"And that," Caelus said quietly, "is why this is dangerous."

Thaloré stepped closer. "Love denied becomes ruthless. We both know this."

"Then tell me what to do," she said, glancing from one brother to the other.

"Do not enter The Chasm yet," Caelus said. "Let us help you plan."

Understanding settled as Eira nodded. She felt confident she could pull this off with her brothers on her side.

"He is searching," Thaloré warned.

"Then we are done," Caelus said. "Go."

Light bent as the realm unraveled, and sound rushed back in around her.

"Eira?" Adrian's voice came from the bedroom.

She turned toward him, expression grim. "I have decided, Adrian. We need to start collecting them."

"The embers," he said, nodding.

"Yes." She closed her eyes briefly, knowing this decision could cost her everything. "I know where a few are. But Adrian—we may not survive this."

"I know," he said, a grin breaking through despite everything. "What is life without a little risk?"

She smiled as she took his hand, feeling a slight weight lift. "We will make this right. Let's go."

The air in the apartment rippled as they stepped forward together.

CHAPTER 22
THE ARCHITECT

Far beyond the mortal realm, beyond the Sovereigns' domains and the slow turning of stars, there existed a place where time did not move forward or back. It did not stretch, compress, or decay. It simply remained—held in a state of careful suspension. Silence lived here, not as emptiness, but as intention. Here, The Architect watched.

He did not observe with eyes, nor with form. He did not sit upon a throne or stand within walls, because there were no walls to contain him and no throne worthy of the task he performed. His awareness was woven into The Loom itself, threaded through every strand of existence, present wherever fate bent or tightened or frayed.

The Loom stretched endlessly before him, a vast expanse of living light. Each thread shimmered with the quiet resonance of a life unfolding—mortal, Sovereign, and those older still. Some burned brightly and briefly. Others glowed with patient persistence. Together, they formed a harmony so complex it bordered on impossible.

For an age uncounted, that harmony had held. Until tonight.

The Architect felt the resistance then. Not absence, not evasion, but deliberate obstruction. A barrier had been raised around their exchange, subtle enough that The Loom did not recoil from it, precise enough that it did not tear. Chaos had learned restraint quickly.

He could feel the outline of it, the pressure where his awareness slid and failed to penetrate fully. Whatever plans were being spoken within it were concealed by design, not chance. That alone narrowed his focus.

Eira was not hiding out of fear—she was hiding with intent. And that registered as a deviation he had not anticipated. He did not take pleasure in correcting what he had made, nor did he hunger for punishment. But Balance was not sentimental. Anything that threatened it would be removed.

The Architect adjusted his attention, testing the barrier without pressing against it. He did not force entry. Force revealed too much, too quickly. Instead, he listened to what bled through despite her control: the tightening of threads, the warming of ember-lines, the subtle alignment of mortal fates that had no reason to draw closer unless guided.

Something was being gathered. Not power in the crude sense, not yet; something quieter, something preparatory. He could not hear the words exchanged between them, but he felt the consequence of those words ripple outward. The Loom responded in hesitant shifts, as though uncertain which future it was being asked to accommodate.

That was new.

The Architect withdrew a fraction of his focus, thoughtful rather than thwarted. Chaos had not shut him out entirely. She had simply denied him certainty. And uncertainty, he knew, was far more dangerous than defiance.

Whatever Eira was planning, it was not reactionary. It was not reckless. It was deliberate. And that, more than her transformation, demanded his attention.

CHAPTER 23
EIRA

The veil wavered ahead of her, thin as breath against glass. Eira slowed as she approached it, her steps faltering—not from doubt, but from the significance pressing beneath her skin and the sharp, unmistakable absence at her back. Adrian had not crossed with her. The space where he should have been felt wrong, like a limb severed mid-motion. She could still feel him through the bond, distant but alive, tethered to the mortal plane she had just left behind. The separation scraped at her nerves, sending turmoil roiling throughout her body.

She had not meant to leave him and panic flared, causing a twisting sensation to stir within her. She wondered if something had happened to prevent his crossing, and that was enough to chill her bones.

Before she could cross, the air changed. Not

sharply or violently, but just enough that the rhythm of the world faltered, like a heart skipping a beat. The light dimmed and a cold presence surrounded her. Eira stopped. She did not need to turn to know who stood behind her.

"Eira," the voice commanded, halting her steps.

She closed her eyes for a brief, treacherous moment, as fear for Adrian sharpened her senses. Then she turned.

Thaloré stood between her and the veil, his presence anchored and immovable. Shadows pooled at his feet like ink spilled from a tipped jar. He wore no armor and carried no weapon. He did not need to. Death had never required such things. The quiet around him was absolute restraint, the hush that came when the world itself understood it should not speak.

She clenched her fists as unease crept through her, cold and unwelcome.

"Move, brother," she said, her tone sharper than she would normally speak to him. "I need to return."

He did not move.

"You cannot pass," Thaloré replied, his voice low and steady, already mourning the action he had not yet taken.

The words struck harder than any blow and Eira's head jerked up, her eyes flashing with fury and hurt combined. "You do not get to decide that, Thaloré," she said, heat bleeding into her tone despite herself.

"I do," he answered gently. "Because I have already watched a world fracture for love once."

Something twisted painfully in her heart. "That is not what this is. You need to let me pass, or I will go through you."

"You could destroy realms, Eira," he said, and for the first time she heard it—the crack beneath his calm. "I am doing what I must."

She took a step forward and the veil shuddered, responding to her presence like a servant recognizing its master.

"Let me pass, Thaloré. I will not say it again." Her voice was calm, lethal. "Please, brother—do not make me move you."

Thaloré did not doubt her. There was no mercy left in her tone, and every word rang with intent.

He did not raise his voice, nor harden his expression. "Eira, I will not let you destroy all of creation to spite The Architect. I know your intention, but I cannot let you carry out this task."

Her breath caught, pain flaring, as his words settled into something that felt like betrayal. "*You* think this is about spite? *You*, of all people?"

"I think grief amplifies power," he said quietly. "And love gives it teeth. Combined with what you are now—only destruction can follow."

She stared at him, disbelief hardening into something colder. "You are stopping me."

The truth settled between them, heavy and irrevocable. His eyes softened and that was what broke her.

"Yes," he said. "I have to, sister."

"No," she whispered. "You wouldn't. You said you would help us." Her voice broke, the words tearing free as the truth settled in.

She stepped closer, tears welling in her eyes. The air around her flared gold, heat spiraling outward as the world bent instinctively toward her will. Chaos surged, answering her pain without hesitation.

Thaloré lifted his hand and shadows surged with it. They wrapped around her without violence and without haste, coiling around her wrists, her throat, her waist. A cocoon of darkness formed around her, so dense it drank the light spilling from her skin. The restraint was absolute. Final.

Her scream tore free anyway. Flames surged outward, brilliant and violent, ripping through the shadows in a burst born not of power, but of betrayal. The eruption shook the air, warped the ground beneath her feet, but it could not touch what had already broken inside her.

Tears streamed down her face, searing hot as they fell, each one dragged from a place she had never learned how to guard. Fury and grief tangled together until she could no longer tell where one ended and the other began. Her breath came in sharp, uneven pulls, as if the world itself had turned against her, constricting her lungs.

"You were my brother," she cried, the words splitting the silence apart. Her voice fractured on the truth, raw with disbelief. "You were the one I trusted! The one I came to when the world was too heavy; when I couldn't carry it alone."

Her hands shook as the flames flared again, answering her pain without judgment. "I believed you," she said, the confession cutting deeper than the accusation. "You said you would stand beside me. Why, Thaloré?"

Realization dawned, and the incredulity staggered her. Her voice broke completely then, the sound stripped of pride, stripped of power.

"And you are the one who decided I was too dangerous to be allowed a choice," she said in a low voice, her eyes flashing with anger.

She gritted her teeth, fists clenching at her sides as fire pulsed beneath her skin. "You *will* let me pass," she said, each word precise and unyielding. "I *will* go back to Adrian."

The fire raged brighter and Thaloré's shadows tightened, but they did not fight her. They only sought to contain. Slowly, inexorably, the flames dimmed—smothered beneath Death's patient hold. Her strength bled away, not stolen, but contained, until her body went slack within the dark.

Thaloré stepped closer. His hand rested against the surface of the shadowed cocoon, as though it were glass and she were something precious breaking beneath it.

"I am sorry," he said, and this time his voice broke. "Caelus and I saw where this path led. I could not let you take it. This is me saving you, Eira."

The world folded and darkness opened—not the violent tearing of space, but a yielding, a soft surrender. The Void received her without hunger and without judgment. A place outside motion, outside time, where Chaos could not burn and grief could not sharpen it.

Eira drifted into it, suspended in perfect, terrible stillness. Her last thought was not of The Architect, nor of Thaloré's betrayal. It was of Adrian—alone, reaching for her across a divide she had never meant to leave between them.

And far above, beyond realms and laws and the trembling Loom, something ancient shifted—not in triumph, not in relief, but in unease. Because Chaos had been caged.

And Chaos never forgets who closed the door.

EPILOGUE- ADRIAN

The moment it happened, Adrian knew. There was no explosion of pain, no dramatic tearing. Just absence where he usually felt her. He stood on the half-lit street where he had anchored himself, senses extended outward the way they always were when Eira moved between realms. He reached for her instinctively, following the familiar pull of her presence.

Nothing answered.

At first, he told himself she had simply shifted too far, slipped into a place his senses could not yet follow. He pushed harder, letting the gold beneath his skin flare, tracing the threads that always led back to her.

There was nothing.

No warmth. No pressure. No distant echo of her power brushing against his awareness.

"Eira!" he yelled, as if this would summon her.

The world did not respond.

Panic surged, cold and immediate. He widened his reach, scanning every layer of reality he could touch—mortal realm, sovereign echoes, and the thin places between. Still nothing.

His chest tightened as he realized she was not hidden nor shielded. She was gone.

"No," he breathed. The word barely existed before his legs gave out, a furious scream ripping free as he hit the concrete. "EIRA!"

The realization struck harder than any blow. He could sense The Loom straining, and knew he would not find her in any realm he knew. He could feel Death's realm distantly, closed to him. But Eira was nowhere.

For the first time since his blood had awakened, Adrian felt truly powerless. He clenched his fists, gold light cracking across his skin.

"I'm coming," he screamed to the empty air, to whatever part of the universe could still hear him. "You don't get to take her from me!"

Chaos stirred within The Void. Eira felt Adrian's fury like a second heartbeat and answered with the smallest piece of herself she could spare from this endless space of nothingness. A single pulse, serving as a promise.

Somewhere in the weave of existence, something ancient cracked—and did not mend.

BONUS CHAPTER- DEATH

When The Void closed around Eira, the world did not react. That was what struck him first. There was no rupture in the fabric of the realms, no shudder of The Loom, no protest from the force she embodied. The veil simply smoothed, the space where she once stood returned to itself as though nothing had been taken. Death always worked this way ... clean and absolute, uninterested in spectacle.

Thaloré remained where he was, his shadows quiet at his feet. Only when his hands began to shake did he realize how tightly he had been holding himself together. He relaxed his fingers slowly, concentrating on his form and the discipline he had honed over eternity.

Eira's anger lingered in him, a memory pressed deep of feelings he had felt centuries ago. He had held her once before, long ago, when Peace had still been learning how to exist in a world that did not know it. He had never imagined that he would one day be the one to bind her.

"I am sorry," he said quietly, though there was no one left to hear him. The words felt thin, even as they left him; apologies always did, when the harm could not be undone.

He turned from the veil at last, each step carrying the dull ache of finality. This was the cost of knowing what lay ahead. The cruelty of foresight was not in seeing disaster, but in understanding that preventing it would still make you a villain in the eyes of the one you loved.

He thought of Caelus then. Of the moment they stood together in his realm deciding on a path they knew would alter everything. They had no choice. Chaos had not simply awakened in Eira. It had aligned with her grief, sharpening into something volatile and immense that could destroy every realm.

"She will choose him," Caelus had said with certainty.

"I know," Thaloré had answered, *"I would have chosen the same path, which is why we must intervene. I know the cost, Caelus. I must bear it for the rest of eternity ... and it is heavy, brother. We cannot let our sister carry that burden or destroy herself in the process."*

They had not spoken for a long time. They did not

need to. The path had already revealed itself, bleak and unavoidable. If Eira crossed back, she would not stop; not out of malice, not even out of rage, but out of love sharpened by anger and fear of losing what she treasured most. Thaloré understood that kind of devotion too well. He had followed it once, defied The Fates for it, and paid the price in a way that had never truly stopped haunting him.

He would not allow her to do the same.

What she was now, could not be allowed to burn unchecked. Chaos answered her pain too readily, and grief had a way of teaching power how to destroy without hesitation. Through Caelus, Thaloré had seen the ending that followed if The Architect intervened. He knew that worlds did not fall screaming. They unraveled quietly, threads snapping one by one, until The Loom deemed it necessary to start a new pattern.

He pressed a fist to his heart, clenching the fabric of his robes. How was he meant to explain that this was mercy? That The Void was not a punishment, but the only place where her power could be stilled long enough for her to survive herself? How could he make her understand that he had chosen her over everything else?

Adrian still lived. Thaloré felt that clearly, the tether of the demigod intact, vibrating with confusion and loss. He did not resent the man. He pitied him.

Love had always been dangerous when it brushed against beings like them.

"I will bear this," Thaloré said into the quiet. "Even if you never forgive me."

This was the role he had accepted long ago. Death did not seek absolution. He stayed behind so others could move forward, made choices no one else would claim, and carried the weight of outcomes that would never be acknowledged.

Far below, in the stillness of The Void, Eira slept suspended outside of time; her grief held in a place where it could not ignite nor destroy the universe.

Thaloré turned away, steadying himself. He knew that loving her enough to stop her might be the most painful duty he would ever fulfill.

Acknowledgements

To my readers—you guys are amazing. Thank you so much for loving the Sovereigns as much as I do!

To my amazing editor, Karen Wendling—Thank you so much for everything that you do! The late night brainstorming, time spent editing, and motivation that you give me to continue writing magical worlds means everything to me! I am so grateful for you!

For everyone who has ever been told they weren't allowed to want more. To take the "safe" path. To follow the same course as everyone else. I hope you didn't listen. I hope you forged your own path, kicked ass, and transformed yourself into someone who takes what they want, defies the norm, and stands unshaken in their beliefs. And most of all— **I hope you gave them hell.**

ABOUT THE AUTHOR

Lana has loved writing since childhood, starting with poetry and growing into full-length stories. A lifelong reader, she gravitates toward fantasy, science fiction, and romance, especially the spicy kind! She has always enjoyed reading and writing fantasy because it lets her dream without limits, create magic, and share that wonder with readers. These genres continue to inspire her storytelling, and she loves building worlds filled with magic, emotion and high stakes. When she isn't writing, Lana enjoys traveling, tending to her plants, and spending time outdoors, where she finds both creativity and calm.

Stay connected! Join my newsletter for exclusive updates, behind-the-scenes content, and first access to new releases.

- instagram.com/lanajwilliamsauthor
- facebook.com/LanaJWilliamsAuthor
- tiktok.com/@thereallanajauthor

www.ingramcontent.com/pod-product-compliance
Lightning Source LLC
LaVergne TN
LVHW021236080526
838199LV00088B/4543